WOLF DECEIVED

ENSNARED BY THE PACK: BOOK 1

TESSA COLE

Gryphon's Gate Publishing

Gryphon's Gate Publishing
550 King St. N.
PO Box 42088 Conestoga
Waterloo, ON
N2L 6K5

Print ISBN: 978-1-990587-04-7

AUDREY

Tonight, my wolf would awaken. It would. Fifth time was the charm, right?

I glanced up, checking the time. The full moon was almost perfectly framed by the large hole in the thick canopy of branches and leaves surrounding the pack's sacred grove, indicating it was only a few minutes until midnight and then— Then! Then I'd become a real shifter.

I nervously ran my hands down the front of my simple white dress. I'd bought the dress on my eighteenth birthday, eager to become an adult in my pack, ready to meet the animal half of my soul even though I knew I'd have to wait ten months before the summer solstice to join the others who'd turned eighteen that year for our first shift.

Except that solstice had come and gone, and my wolf still hadn't woken.

A part of me wished our pack was like the other packs, born with our animal natures fully awake, shifting around six or seven years old whenever we wanted and not needing to wait until our eighteenth birthday. But then I would have had sixteen or seventeen years of being the laughingstock of my pack and not just five.

Instead, centuries ago, the then pack alpha paid a witch to halt our transformation until we were eighteen. It was a way to protect ourselves from being discovered by the humans and it had made us a significant pack in North America. We'd been able to build our own village out in the open instead of hiding away from the humans and gain influence and prosperity in a world that would have hunted us down if they'd known the truth.

Then a little over twenty-five years ago, Michael had tried to exterminate every human on the planet — as well as all of us hidden supernatural beings — and Gabriel made a deal with every super in hiding to join the fight.

The deal had turned the tide of the war, and the need to hide, to avoid children losing control and shifting in front of a human, no longer mattered. The world knew about shifters and vampires and demons and angels. We were the heroes that had helped save humanity, and now we were the pack that couldn't shift until we were adults.

And I was the girl who couldn't shift at all.

But this year would be different. I could feel it.

This was my year.

The full moon was a good sign. Those who awakened

under the full moon were said to be stronger, more connected with their wolves.

This year my wolf would awaken and I'd become an adult and get the hell out of this town. Not that I technically wasn't an adult at twenty-two — at least according to the humans — but as far as pack law was concerned, I was still a child.

On top of that, once my wolf wakened, I wouldn't look like a target to every supernatural being I came across the moment I left pack land, since while my essence told every super who saw me that I was a shifter, it also told them I was so weak I was practically human.

Merrick, our pack's alpha, wouldn't be able to use any of that as an excuse to keep me here any longer. Although I had a bad feeling he'd find some other excuse. No money, no family, no something I'd never been able to have in the first place. I was free labor, and according to him I *owed* him for taking me in when my father killed himself thirteen years ago.

He always told me he could have let someone else take me, but no, my father had been a valued member of the pack even after he'd come back from the war broken and haunted by the things he'd experienced, and Merrick had been obligated to take care of *family*.

That, of course, had been a lie, but I'd been too young to realize the truth until it was too late. Not that I'd have been able to do anything about it.

No one defied the alpha, especially someone who was still considered a child.

Joan and Shea, with their perfectly coifed blond locks, stepped into the sacred clearing with their younger siblings who'd turned eighteen a few months ago, and a chill rushed through me as my pulse picked up.

I inched back toward the deeper shadows of the grove where the pale moonlight didn't reach and tried to make myself look smaller, even though I knew I wouldn't be able to hide from their enhanced night vision unless I was in complete shadow. But it was the best I could do. I had to be here for the ceremony so I couldn't just run away.

Hopefully they wouldn't notice me and everything would be fine. They were here for their siblings, not me. But their attention instantly jumped to me as if they'd been looking for me and it didn't matter if I made myself smaller or not.

Joan sneered, catching me trying to will myself invisible, and my pulse pounded faster. Sometimes it worked. Sometimes when I couldn't just flee, I managed to hide in the shadows and not be noticed, but I should have known they'd search me out. I was guaranteed to be here. I was tonight's amusement. And now I looked like prey. Prey that Joan had been toying with for years.

She'd had her eye on Sterling, Merrick's son and my sort of — definitely unwanted — brother since we were little. She'd been furious when I'd moved into his house, her tormenting reaching new heights that had often sent me to the nurse's office until she'd realized I'd actually become Sterling's slave. Then they'd joined forces, honing their skills to make my *accidents* look more like accidents and learning that waiting for an attack elicited as big or bigger a reaction than actually being attacked.

God, I should have just run when I'd started fantasizing about it years ago.

I certainly should have done it after the first summer solstice when I didn't shift.

I should have stolen what I could have easily carried so I could pawn it in the next town over and taken the bus as far away from here as possible, like to Union City. That was on the other side of the country and had a whole vibrant supernatural quarter. Surely the wolf pack there would take me in. I'd become damn good at cooking and cleaning, so I at least had a few useful skills.

Except it didn't matter where I went, Merrick would find me. As soon as it came out that I was a shifter who couldn't shift he'd know where I was because there wasn't anyone else out there like me. And yeah, I'd spent the last five years back in my old high school's library at their one remaining clunky student computer, searching the internet for anything that might tell me why I couldn't shift.

"Every time you show up you just prove the rumors true," Shae snickered with a wicked gleam in her eyes that made my pulse race even faster because she knew I couldn't refuse the ritual until I actually shifted. "You're just a mutt. Not even shifter enough to have a wolf. Your mom fucked a human and your dad was too stupid to know the truth."

Except I had proof that wasn't the reason I couldn't shift. There wasn't such a thing as a half shifter. Children of human-shifter pairings were either shifters with the ability to shift and the essence of a shifter, or human with the essence of a human. There was no in between like me.

Joan barked a shrill laugh, and her younger sister and Shae's younger brother joined in.

"Stupid must run in the family," Joan cackled, her voice rising and drawing the attention of the two dozen others in the grove. Not that she needed to speak up. Shifters had excellent senses — smell, sight, and hearing — once their animal-soul had awakened. "You're never going to shift."

"I think we should change the ritual this year," Sterling purred as he slunk out of the shadows and drew up close behind me, making me jump. His ferocious power rolled over me, threatening to dominate me and force me to my knees in submission just by being near me, and I realized he'd fully suppressed his power to sneak up and surprise me. "I think we should make the mutt run when she doesn't shift."

AUDREY

A SHUDDER SWEPT THROUGH ME AS I FOUGHT TO KEEP standing and not kneel in front of Sterling like his power demanded. They'd made that threat before and followed through with an incident that had left me limping for weeks. I'd thought once they'd become adults the bullying would stop, that they'd get on with their lives, but I'd been wrong. I was too much fun and with their animal natures fully heightened, they used me to hone their new hunting abilities.

Sterling nicked a claw against the back of my neck with a sharp sting and sauntered over to Joan as I slapped my hand over the wound.

The warm blood oozing from the cut coated my palm. It wasn't deep, but it wasn't a papercut, either. Swell.

It would heal when I shifted… if I shifted—

No. I *would* shift tonight. But until then, I'd draw even more unwanted attention.

He cocked a pale eyebrow and smirked, the look doing nothing to diminish his striking appearance. He was a devil in an angel's skin, blond, beautiful, with a naturally sculpted physique, and a cruel speck of black nothingness for a heart. He knew full well that he'd made it so that if I didn't shift, the newly awakened wolves, with their predatory senses suddenly on overdrive from being repressed, might see me as prey and attack instead of going on the run with the alpha, and there was nothing I could do about it.

Joan sniffed sharply and sneered, her lips curling back revealing her extended canines. "She always smells like prey."

Shae inched closer to me, her eyes darkening as her wolf's nature rose closer to the surface, her hunger clear in her expression. Even her brother and Joan's sister, on the verge of awakening their wolf but not yet wolves, drew closer, their noses working, picking up the scent of my blood.

My pulse roared and I fought the urge to hug myself.

Don't look like prey. Don't. Or at least not any more than you already do. Stay. Calm.

But I wouldn't put it past them to double back after the shift took over the newest adults of the pack and that thought terrified me.

Merrick and our packs' beta would lead their first run, but those who'd already shifted didn't have to join in and didn't have to stay with the group like the newly made adults did. And if I didn't shift, I was a target just waiting to be attacked.

"If you kill her, who will clean your house?" Royce asked.

A hint of his power rolled over me as he stepped out of the shadows on the other side of the circle and sauntered toward the group, but then he pulled it back completely like he always did when he was around Sterling, like a good beta should. His eyes were just as dark as the others, his wolf close to taking over, but his expression remained flat, not hungry, and I was almost relieved to see him.

Almost, because he'd never attacked me or put me down. Of course, he'd also never publicly gone against Sterling to stop him. As far as everyone was concerned, he was on team Sterling. Like almost everyone else. He had, however, since that first year when I hadn't shifted, been making little comments to protect me and subtly distracting Sterling and Joan so I could slip away before things got out of hand. And while he'd been doing it for four years, I still had no idea what to make of it.

"Of course, when her wolf wakes tonight, you'll need to find a new housecleaner regardless. She'll be an adult and able to move out of your house. You know," Royce added with a pointed look at Sterling, "that thing kids do when they become adults."

"There's no point in moving out of my father's house. It'll be mine soon," Sterling huffed, jumping right to Royce's jab about still living at home. "And she'd still be an unmated female with ties to the alpha. Dad will want her to stay until he can find her a suitable match."

My thoughts lurched at that. "He what?"

Had Sterling just implied that Merrick was going to arrange who my mate was?

Everyone's attention snapped to me. The force of their ferocious natures pressed against my senses, and I froze.

Crap. One wrong move and their wolves would take over and they'd attack. Or rather they'd *let* their wolves take over.

"Your mate would have influence over the alpha. You *are* my sister," Sterling said even though he'd made a point over the years to remind me that I wasn't his sister. "Every male in the pack knows that."

But that was just another excuse. I didn't have any power and everyone in the pack knew it. The only way I could get power was if my mate was powerful. Of course, that was if I stayed. If I left... yeah, the odds of me having power in a different pack were slim, too, but that was better than being here.

"Dad probably won't even wait for your wolf," Sterling said. "You're old enough. You need a good match. One that looks good for our pack. Since by pack law you're still a child, it'll be up to him to find you a suitable mate."

He flashed me a wicked smile, wrapped an arm around Joan's waist, and led her, Shae, and their younger siblings away.

My heart slammed inside me, no doubt audible to everyone around me. Would Merrick let me leave even if my wolf woke this evening?

I'd be an adult. He'd have to.

Now my wolf had to show up. It wasn't the dark ages and our pack didn't have arranged matings, but I wouldn't put it past Merrick to use me as political leverage. He was pissed that his wife had left him for a human and pissed that our pack no longer had the same political influence over the other North American packs that it used to have.

And he was really pissed that he hadn't been asked to be the North American shifter representative in the Joined Parliament where supers governed pretty much the whole supernatural world. There was no way he'd sacrifice his precious heir with an arranged mating to improve his position among the other packs, which left me as the sacrificial offering to his political goals.

AUDREY

As if thinking about him made him appear, Merrick strode into the sacred grove. My attention, along with everyone else's, jumped to him. Even with his ferocious power only partially released, it still crackled against my senses and thickened the air. It didn't press against me, willing me to my knees like Sterling's had, but that was only because he wasn't trying to exert his will on us.

He reached the center of the grove and the group closed around him, ready to begin the ritual. Everyone about to meet the wolf-half of their soul was dressed in white, while everyone else was stripping out of their clothes since the nature of our magic that allowed us to shift completely destroyed whatever we wore.

For those of us about to be adults — *please, oh please let me become an adult tonight* — the destruction of our white clothing symbolized our transformation from child to adult. For everyone else, it was better on the bank account to strip first instead of constantly having to buy new clothing.

"It's an auspicious night," Merrick said, his voice a deep rumble as he turned his attention to the moon and I kept mine on him, determined not to see something I didn't want to see — like Sterling naked. "Wolves that wake under the full moon are leaders in our community. Much will be expected of you."

The eleven teens about to take their first transformation into adulthood drew closer, stepping into the circle of moonlight.

"You're so sure your wolf won't wake that you're not going to join them?" Royce asked, suddenly right beside me, his voice low.

"My wolf can wake just fine over here," I hissed back, fighting the urge to glance at him.

He'd played this game with me before. Two years ago, he'd come up beside me during the ritual and I'd gotten an eyeful of his honed physique and semi-hard cock. I was sure my eyes had bulged out of my head as my face had burned with embarrassment.

I knew it was stupid. Shifters were naked all the time.

Except our pack *wasn't* naked all the time. We were essentially humans with aggressive tendencies until we were eighteen and because I had yet to shift, I hadn't been involved in any of the hunts or games.

The only times I'd seen anyone naked was that one time I'd accidentally walked in on Sterling in the bathroom — and gotten my arm broken for my mistake —

and the four other times I'd attended the transformation ceremony. But during the ceremony it had been night and hard to see much of anything unless someone had been standing right beside me, like Royce had... and now was.

"Audrey," he murmured, his voice strangely soft, surprising me and straining my control to keep my attention on Merrick in the center of the grove. "Tonight's your night. I can feel it."

I huffed a bitter laugh despite my hope that my wolf would wake tonight. "Yeah, because I'm supposed to be a leader in our community?"

"Why wouldn't you be?"

Because no one would listen to me. I was the girl who couldn't shift, the girl who scrubbed floors like Cinderella and was about to have a prearranged mating like a woman from the Dark Ages. And no, there was no Prince Charming or fairy godmother who was going to give me a happily ever after. Happily ever after didn't happen in real life.

Except the moment I thought that, I thought of Mila and her fated mate. She'd heard the power of a rare fated mating call with a shifter from another pack and had left town last year. We'd grown up together, her friendship never wavering even after Sterling, Joan, and their friends ramped up their bullying. She'd tried to resist the call, put off being with her mate, but it had made her miserable. I hadn't wanted her to leave, but I also didn't want to stand in the way of her happily ever after, so, after a lot of promising that I'd join her new pack the minute my wolf woke, she'd left.

She had a happily ever after. Maybe I had a fated mate as well. If I had one, Merrick couldn't arrange my mating and my mate might be able to protect me from Sterling, or better yet, he'd be from a different pack like Mila's mate.

Which was childish wishful thinking. A man wasn't going to solve my problems and really, what kind of pathetic woman would I be if I hoped a man would whisk me off my feet and rescue me?

A tired, scared woman with very few options, a tiny voice said inside me.

But a fated mate just wasn't in my cards. Just like my wolf awakening probably wasn't either. And if I was going to be free of Sterling and his fan club, I was going to have to take matters into my own hands.

I bit back a sigh and focused all my attention on Merrick and the others in the middle of the grove. Merrick pulled off his shirt, preparing to shift, and the group inched closer, drawn by his power.

I felt the tug as well, a tightening in my chest, but I stayed where I was. If I didn't shift, I didn't want a new, possibly out-of-control wolf to notice that I'd been bleeding and possibly still was.

He chanted the Ritual of Welcoming and Transformation and the pressure in my chest grew stronger. But this wasn't a precursor to my wolf waking, just the alpha evoking the magic that would allow the wolf half of our soul to wake.

The pressure had happened the previous four solstices. The first time I'd thought I was really going to shift. The second time I was hopeful. Now I knew something else needed to happen. I just had no idea what.

Then searing agony exploded in my chest, stealing my breath and dropping me to my knees.

This was it. I was going to shift. My wolf was going to wake and I could get the hell out of this town.

But the pain was blinding, unlike anything I'd experienced before, and my sudden joy that I was finally going to be a real shifter snapped to panic.

This wasn't how a shift was supposed to feel. Shifting was natural to our kind, our body turned to liquid and reformed in our animal form, as easy as breathing. It didn't hurt and it certainly didn't feel like I was being burned alive and ripped apart from the inside.

I clenched my jaw, fighting the agony, desperate to not draw attention to myself, especially in such a vulnerable position on my hands and knees. Sterling would use this weakness against me, probably use it as proof that I was never going to shift and Merrick needed to find me a mate before everyone in the other packs realized the truth. Although how he'd explain my complete lack of power to anyone looking at me and not mention that I couldn't shift was beyond me.

"What do you know, she is a shifter?" Joan snickered.

"She isn't if it hurts," Sterling replied, pushing away from his father and striding toward me.

He grabbed my ponytail and yanked my head back as another explosion ripped through me, this one with a deafening gong that reverberated through my whole body.

"Let her go," Royce snarled, grabbing Sterling's wrist and twisting, breaking his hold on me.

"Fuck off," Sterling shot back, his power flaring, crushing against me, demanding I bow down to him.

He reached for me again, but Royce shoved him before he could grab hold, and he stumbled back.

"Stay away from her," Royce growled, kneeling beside me.

My gaze leaped up to his, shocked that he'd defend me against his best friend in public. There was no going back from that. Sterling would be pissed, and Royce had just lost his chance at being pack beta when Sterling took over from his father.

But then our eyes met and all my thoughts vanished, burned away by the power roaring and clanging inside me, and I was falling falling falling into his dark eyes.

They were bottomless and consuming and filled with power. He wasn't as strong as Sterling, couldn't command the same number of shifters to the same degree, but he still had the potential to crush me with a howl. And yet I knew he wouldn't.

Because he was mine.

My mate.

His eyes widened and the fire swept back into my chest, leaving my limbs and face cold, but I was barely aware of it, of anything. We might not have known each other very well, but once we did, we'd be in love forever. That was how fated mating bonds worked. They were precious and rare, a strange side effect of the spell that had taken away our ability to shift until we were eighteen, and those with fated mate bonds were revered among the pack.

I did have a happily ever after.

And Royce had a high enough status in the pack that even if Sterling chose someone else to be his primary beta when he took over, I'd still be safe from their torments. Sterling would lose face if he continued to pick on me. I was no longer the girl who killed her mother just by being born, or whose father had killed himself, or who couldn't shift.

I was now the girl with a fated mate.

AUDREY

Sterling growled low and opened his mouth to say something, but his father barked his name.

"He's not your beta if he defies you. He never was," Merrick said.

Around him, the adults were shifting, their bodies transforming in a quick, fluid motion from one shape to another, starting on two legs and ending on four. Ripples rolled through a few of the teens, their forms shuddering, solidifying back to human, then shuddering again. The wolves beside them drew closer, offering support with physical contact while Merrick shifted, raised his head to the moon, and released a long, deafening howl.

Awaken and run.

Power rolled through the grove and those teens whose forms were already starting to change dropped to their hands and knees and shifted. The others started to lose their form and Merrick howled again.

His alpha's command, to take my true form, to wake and run, squeezed inside me. I had to obey. I wanted to obey. I was pack — and I sure as hell wasn't even close to being an alpha and able to resist his power.

But just like the last four years, no matter how much I wanted to obey, nothing inside me responded to his call, not a growl or huff or a sense that my body had the capability of being anything other than human.

My throat tightened with disappointment, but I pushed it aside. I wasn't done yet. My wolf could still wake. I could still shift. I just needed to try harder, concentrate more, something, anything.

Awaken, Merrick roared in my head, as if he knew I needed another stronger push to shift.

His golden gaze seized me from across the grove and the pressure crushed around my heart.

I fought to breathe, to will my body into transforming. Please. This was my year. I was going to shift. I had to shift. Even with a fated mate, I wanted to shift. I wanted to be what I'd been born to be. A wolf shifter, a supernatural being, a predator, not some helpless prey who wasn't shifter enough to be a super but not human enough to be human, either.

I squeezed my eyes shut and searched inside myself for even just a spark of ferociousness, a flicker of animalistic power, something, anything.

But there was only me. There had only ever been me. Weak, fragile, so close to human I should have just been born human.

Pathetic, Merrick huffed inside my head. He turned away from me and released another howl. The rest of the group responded and they took off into the woods, leaving me panting against the pressure that remained in my chest, my soul aching and empty.

Did I even have a wolf? How many times could I come to the grove on the summer solstice and not shift before I accepted the truth?

I was a shifter who couldn't shift.

I *was* pathetic.

I pressed my forehead to the forest floor, gasping in ragged breaths, the deep musty scent of dirt doing nothing to steady me and ground me within my body because I didn't want to be where I was. I didn't want to be aching and empty in our pack's sacred grove. I wanted to be running through the forest with the other wolves. I wanted to be recognized as an adult, hell, even just a person.

My eyes burned and my throat tightened with tears I didn't want to shed. Crying was weak. Except I *was* weak. Sterling was right. He'd always been right. I was prey and would always be prey.

And I needed to remember that and get home before Sterling, Joan, and Shae could double back and attack me and—

No. They wouldn't because Royce still knelt beside me. They might not have figured out yet that he'd protected me because of our fated mating call, but they knew something was up, and they'd figure it out soon enough. Then Royce would join me as the laughingstock of the pack. Mated to the shifter who couldn't shift.

I cracked my eyes open and glanced at him, my forehead still pressed against the cool uneven ground, too tired to bother raising my head. He hadn't touched me or said anything the whole time, but from his expression it looked more like he wasn't sure how to approach me instead of horrified that I was his fated mate.

"So much for this year being my year," I said.

"I don't know," he said with a shrug. "How many of us can say we've heard a fated mating call?"

He offered me a soft smile. It lit up his face and I was struck with how handsome he was. Compared to Sterling in his shining captain-of-the-football-team blond glory, Royce with his spikey brown hair and muddy brown eyes hadn't stood out as good looking. He'd been handsome, but nothing compared to his friend. But his smile, so real and comforting, turned him into an angel and it was breathtaking. I wasn't sure I'd ever seen him smile like that.

The thought sent whispering heat teasing down my spine. This was a smile just for me. His mate.

"Well of the current group available, I'd say a hundred percent of us can say we've heard a fated mating call," I replied with a soft laugh.

He rolled his eyes at me. "Your sample size is too small. Two isn't enough for anything. Well…" He coughed and glanced away. "It's enough for ah… something else."

"Like completing the mating bond?" I wasn't sure how

I felt about that even knowing that was the next step for us.

Yes, Royce was my fated mate and I couldn't pretend I hadn't heard the call. I hadn't thought it would come with an explosive fire that would make me feel like I was being burned alive — Mila hadn't said anything about that — but we knew so little about the call that everyone's call could be different. Perhaps the magic needed for my and Royce's souls to recognize each other had to be stronger because I was a broken shifter.

On the other hand, completing the bond meant having sex with someone I barely knew. Not that knowing him would change anything. We'd still be fated mates. I'd just hoped I'd be a little less self-conscious about the whole sex thing before I actually had sex. Especially since I'd never actually *had* sex before. It had been hard enough to keep Mila as a friend and next to impossible to find a guy to have any kind of relationship with.

And while I knew I was going to have to admit that to Royce before we completed our bond and he probably wouldn't judge me, I wasn't prepared for the look he'd give me when he realized I was a virgin.

"How about coffee first?" I suggested as I pushed up to my feet and leaned against a tree to steady myself.

"I'd love to," he said, standing as well, his hands reaching for me as if to help me with my balance but stopping before making contact, still uncertain of himself. "But I don't think we can afford to wait. Not even for coffee." He glanced across the grove in the direction the pack had gone. "Sterling wasn't lying when he said Merrick was going to arrange a mating for you. I overheard the alpha on the phone the other day. He's going to send you to the Albuquerque pack."

"Albuquerque?" I was surprised he wasn't sending me to Union City or to a pack in Europe. Albuquerque wasn't close, but it wasn't exactly far away, either. Except getting rid of me wasn't the plan. Using me as currency to buy what he wanted was, and if that was the case— "Isn't the Albuquerque alpha the head of the North American Shifter Alliance?"

"And they just had a seat open up at the table," Royce said. "It's not the JP, but it's the next best thing."

"Does he honestly think the alpha will give him that seat once he learns he's been sent a defective shifter?" It didn't make sense, not for something like that. But then if he wasn't going to mate me to a shifter for his own political gain, why would he arrange a mating for me?

"It sounded like it didn't matter whether you could shift or not," Royce said.

My pulse picked up. I really didn't like the implications of that. The Albuquerque pack had a renowned supernatural research facility and if Merrick wasn't shipping me off to be someone's wife, he could be shipping me off to find out why I was a shifter who couldn't shift. And I didn't want to think about how they were going to gather their data.

"We can't risk Merrick denying our bond," Royce

added, inching closer to me and reaching a tentative hand to cup my cheek.

My pulse fluttered at his touch and at the desperate look in his eyes. I leaned into his palm and warmth billowed in my chest and radiated over my cheek where our flesh met.

God, it felt so good to be touched. Since Mila had left, there hadn't been anyone to satisfy my shifter need for physical contact, and I hadn't realized just how much I missed it until now.

"He can't deny a fated mating call," I replied, my voice turning breathy and the heat in my chest sinking low within me, the need to seal our bond rising even though it had only just been awakened. "Even if we haven't said our vows and completed the bond, we're still fated mates."

His gaze dipped to my lips and the heat blossomed into an achy need. What would it feel like to kiss him? What would it be like to do more? Unlike me, I was sure he'd had practice, had kissed someone, probably a few someones, before. He'd probably *been* with a woman, too.

And now I was even more self-conscious of the fact that I'd never been intimate with someone.

"I don't want to bet on Merrick respecting a fated mating call," Royce murmured, inching even closer, his breath feathering across my lips. "I never thought I'd have a fated mate and I'm not going to lose you before I even know you."

The need and fear in his eyes matched mine. Merrick

couldn't be trusted. He'd use me however he saw fit and the only way to guarantee that didn't happen was to seal my mating bond with Royce.

"Okay," I breathed. "Take me to your place."

"Sterling could still catch us before we get there." Royce brushed his lips against mine. Desire shivered all the way down my body, inflaming the aching need between my thighs. "Let's do it here in the sacred grove under the summer solstice's full moon."

AUDREY

"Okay," I said again, unable to come up with another word, unable to think past the knowledge that I was about to seal a mating bond with someone let alone my fated mate.

My heart pounded as Royce slipped his hand behind my back, tugged me close against his naked body, and captured my lips in a scorching kiss. It was strong and powerful and overwhelming.

I gasped at the ferocity of his passion and he slipped his tongue into my mouth, teasing me, adding to the fiery mating call within me that was about to explode once again into an inferno of desire.

I tangled my fingers in his hair, clinging to him, gasping for breath, dizzy against his onslaught. His cock, trapped between our bodies, hardened, proof of his desire for me, fueling my need and my certainty that this was right.

"God, Audrey," he growled against my lips. "Say your vow so I can say mine and we can be together."

"Blessed be the moon and her children," I said.

He nipped at my lips and reached under the skirt of my dress, sliding his hands up my thighs to cup my bare ass — since I hadn't wanted to destroy one of my few pairs of underwear shifting — and pressed his length against me.

"And blessed be this sacred vow," I continued, my voice getting breathier by the second.

He rolled his hips, rubbing himself against me through my dress and ratcheting up my need.

The fated mating call rang again, louder this time than before. It vibrated through me, a powerful, deep, resounding *gong* filled with certainty that drowned out everything else. Royce was my mate. We belong together. We would always be together. We—

"I answer the call—" Royce prompted, reminding me that I needed to finish the vow and awaken the binding magic that joined two shifters' souls together so Royce could say his vow and we could seal our bond.

"I answer the call and join my soul with you, my mate," I finished. "My *fated* mate," I corrected myself.

The call rang again, and the need and heat that had awakened with the fated mating call ignited every cell in my body. I was going to change a part of my essence, bind it to my mate in a way only two shifters could bind themselves together, and that meant calling on a primal magic that affected the very core of my being.

"Perfect," Royce purred, his tone suddenly cold and dark, making my thoughts trip.

That wasn't what he was supposed to say. He was supposed to—

He grabbed my ponytail and jerked my head back, holding it at a painful angle.

"Royce, that hurts." I squirmed in his grip, but he held tight and glared down at me, his face a mask of dark satisfaction and malice. The love and hope and fear that Merrick would deny our mating was completely gone. There was no indication that he'd heard the call, that he wanted to take the sacred vows with me and seal our bond. "Royce—"

"About time," Sterling said, jerking my attention from Royce's cold eyes to him. He sauntered naked from the shadows on the other side of the grove, directly in my line of sight as if he didn't want me to miss seeing him, his lips curled back in a wicked smile. "Did you have to play with her first?"

Royce spat on the ground by our feet and wiped his mouth with the back of his free hand. "She needed to believe the call was real so she'd say the vow."

"The call wasn't real?" How could a fated mating call not be real? It was fate, two perfectly aligned souls finding each other. It couldn't be faked.

"Of course it wasn't, mutt," Sterling said. "Pay a witch enough and you can get a spell to do anything."

But it had to be real. It *felt* real.

Royce had protected me from Sterling, publicly

defied him. He wouldn't have done that if he wasn't my fated mate. I needed him. Everything in my soul said we belonged together. "You're lying. It's real. You feel it." I turned to Royce. "You have to feel it. We're fated mates. We—"

Royce jerked my head back farther, sending sharp pain slicing through my scalp. "You honestly think my fated mate would be a wolf who can't even shift?"

"But I felt it." I clawed at his hand, desperate to break his hold. His words cut into my soul and the power of the incomplete mating bond heaved inside me, urging me to seal it.

Be with him. He's our mate. It's real. Real!

I didn't know how I'd gone from one minute determined to leave the pack the second my wolf woke — or didn't wake this evening — to desperately needing Royce. It didn't make sense. But the desire to seal my bond with him was overwhelming. It consumed me, thrumming and burning, begging for completion. It had to be real.

"I heard the call," I gasped. "It was real."

"Fuck she's stupid, isn't she?" Sterling spat as he uncovered a vial with a red glowing liquid from his pile of clothes.

"And pathetic," Royce snarled, wrenching me up by my hair until my toes skimmed the ground, his greater shifter strength more than enough to lift my weight with one hand. "You're a shame to this pack and I can't believe Merrick let you live after your first solstice when you didn't shift. We'd never be mates."

I clung to his wrist, trying to hold myself up, my bare feet skittering over the moss, trying to find enough footing to support my weight. My thoughts whirled and stuttered, the compulsion from the newly formed bond tearing into me as horrible realization hit me. The incomplete vow was why I suddenly couldn't live without someone I barely knew, why I couldn't let him go when only minutes ago I'd been perfectly fine without him. I'd started the magic to seal our bond and it was now compelling me to finish.

I had to fight it, refute it now before it completely took over. Sure, if Royce didn't complete his half of the bond, it would eventually fade, but that could take months, possibly years, and I was *not* going to spend any time pining over someone who didn't love me.

"Why?" I gasped, straining to focus past the clawing need threatening to tear me apart.

I needed him.

No. I was strong enough without him.

But you can't shift. You're not a wolf. You're nothing but prey.

"You're sick," I forced out. *And I love you.*

No. I. Don't.

"How could you manipulate the calling like that?"

Come on. Concentrate. Refute it.

"Because I needed someone with an incomplete mating bond," Sterling said with a sneer before striding to the center of the grove. "I'm going to make our pack powerful again, but I needed a sacrifice." And from the look in his eyes, that *sacrifice* involved something horrible and he was more than happy to sacrifice me.

Oh no.

Oh no no no.

I heaved and clawed against Royce's grip. "Let me go."

"It's like you were made to be our pack's sacrifice," Sterling continued as Royce wrenched me toward the center of the grove, his steps even, unaffected by my flailing. "No one will miss you and you don't even have a wolf. You're not really a member of this pack."

"Mila will miss me," I said.

Come on. Refute the bond and break the magic. He'd said he needed an incomplete mating bond so if I severed the magic empowering it, he wouldn't be able to sacrifice me.

But I couldn't get my thoughts to focus to work up enough willpower to break the magic. I needed Royce. I didn't want to die. How the fuck had no one noticed Sterling was insane?

"Mila is too busy with her *fated* mate," Royce chuckled, his tone for *fated* mocking, twisting my need for him tighter which only deepened my disgust at myself. How could I have been so stupid? No one would be a fated mate to a shifter who couldn't shift. I should have known something wasn't right from the very beginning.

"It's a shame the guy we picked for her turned out to be half decent," Sterling replied, turning my aching desire and screaming frustration into a sudden, fearful cold.

They'd manipulated Mila just like they'd manipulated me? Her guy wasn't her fated mate? For all I knew she didn't have a fated mate, either. I had to warn her that her mate was manipulating her. Except he'd happily taken his vows with her and completed their bond, and I hadn't sensed that he didn't love her... of course I hadn't sensed that Royce was deceiving me, either.

"Yeah, well, we couldn't risk bringing someone else in on our plan," Royce said. "He had to be just as oblivious as the bitches."

They laughed as if it was the funniest thing in the world to mess with someone's emotions while Sterling poured the glowing red contents in his vial on the ground and hissed a few sharp words I didn't recognize.

Magic exploded around us. It slammed into me, stealing my breath, and roared into a wild black whirling mist that shot up from the ground and poured into the sky turning into thick black clouds that blotted out the moon.

"All right, god of power," Sterling yelled. "Accept our sacrifice and show yourself."

AUDREY

Lightning sliced through the clouds and black misty tendrils rushed around me, digging into my essence, seizing the pressure and heat in my chest from the incomplete mating bond and yanking on it, trying to pull it from my body.

Oh, shit.

I mentally scrambled to hold it in and break the magic. He couldn't complete the sacrifice if he didn't have an incomplete bond.

"I refute him!" I screamed into the vortex, heaving against Royce's grip. "I refute this asshole. I take it all back."

"Too late, mutt," Royce snarled. "The god has you bound and he's about to eat you alive."

"No." I tried to knee him in the groin, but he turned to the side and my knee skimmed his hip instead, so I rammed my heel down his shin, drawing a snarl of pain.

"Fucking bitch," he roared and backhanded me.

The impact broke my nose and shot agony through my face. Blood gushed down my chin and splattered on the ground. A brilliant flash of lightning streaked from the clouds and blasted into the center of the grove with a resounding *boom*.

"Come and take your sacrifice," Sterling called out.

More of my blood splattered on the ground followed by another blast of lightning and roar of thunder.

"I refute you. I refute you," I gasped. *Please, I refute you.*

The incomplete bond trembled and chilled. I was doing it. Just a little more and this would all be over. Sterling and Royce would be pissed, I'd have to fight for my life to escape, but the assholes wouldn't get whatever it was they wanted.

"I refute you!" I yelled

"And he doesn't care." Royce's fingers turned to claws and he tore through my dress and dug deep gouges in my chest.

Agony sliced through me, a mix of physical and magical pain, and I screamed. The incomplete mating bond ripped into my soul deeper and more painful than Royce's claws ripping into my flesh. The magic still thought he was my fated mate, and the pain of my mate's attack was overwhelming, stealing every thought but the desperate one to run. *Run now. Now!*

The lightning crackled and roared, illuminating the grove brighter than daylight and filling the air with the reek of ozone. Then the black mist burst apart, revealing an enormous column of rippling air, like heat rolling off asphalt on a summer's day, and radiating an enormous, crushing power.

Royce threw me to the ground at Sterling's feet, and a large red clawed hand reached out of the rippling air. It grabbed me, the claws piercing my back and chest, adding to the agony wracking my body, and the creature hoisted me up as it stepped fully out of the ripple.

It looked like a greater demon with large, leathery wings, fangs, and ram's horns protruding from his forehead. But it was bigger. A lot bigger. Which meant it was enormous since greater demons were already some of the largest supers in all the realms. It also didn't radiate any heat like a demon, let alone the enormous amount of heat that a greater demon was said to radiate with its essence fully released, and every inch of its skin — save for whatever lay under its loincloth — was red like a bad movie version of the devil where greater demons looked more-or-less human.

"She's weak, but she smells delicious," the monster snarled, revealing a mouth full of sharp teeth, "like sorrow and desperation." His tongue flicked out, swiping through the gashes Royce had carved into my breasts, lapping at my blood.

Oh God, oh God, oh God.

I wrenched in the monster's grip, driving its claws deeper into my body, my fear consuming all pain as well as all logic. I was pinned in its grasp, flailing wouldn't free me, but I had to do something. I was *not* going to be eaten by some monster. No way in hell.

Then a wave of power coming from somewhere behind me crashed over me with the command to kneel, crushing my insides because I couldn't move.

Sterling and Royce did drop to the ground and Merrick stormed into the grove.

"You broke into my safe and summoned it?" Merrick roared. "You idiot. He'll kill us all."

"He'll make us strong," Sterling shot back and he lunged at his father, somehow defying the alpha's power that was still squeezing my insides.

Merrick jerked out of the way, his eyes wide, likely with surprise that Sterling was strong enough to defy his power, but Sterling moved with him and rammed both sets of his claws into Merrick's chest. The alpha grunted in pain and slashed at Sterling's back, but Sterling ducked down, tearing his claws through Merrick's belly, and dancing out of the way.

Blood gushed onto the ground, and Merrick grabbed his stomach in a weak attempt to stop the bleeding. But the wound was too deep, eight long gashes that practically opened him up. Even with his heightened healing ability and the ability to heal by shifting, the injury was too great. Shifting now would just kill him. He needed to get to a hospital.

"Even better," the monster roared. "More power and more desperation." It tossed me aside like a discarded doll and dove on the wounded alpha.

I slammed into a tree, pitched forward, hit another tree with my head, and crashed in a heap on the ground, the world spinning around me.

Through my wavering vision, I watched the demon shove his hand into Merrick's gut, rip something out, and eat it.

Merrick screamed and my stomach heaved. That was going to be me—

That could still be me.

Merrick might be the main course now, but I could still be dessert. I had to get up and run.

I heaved up to my hands and knees. Darkness swam across my vision, but I forced myself to keep going, grabbed the tree beside me, and climbed to my feet, sending another wave of darkness that threatened my consciousness.

The monster howled in delight, catching my attention and giving me a perfect, horrific view of it drawing another strangled cry by tearing off Merrick's arm and chomping on it like a chicken wing.

My stomach heaved again and I staggered to the next tree, deeper into the forest and the shadows. I moved to the next and the next, the sounds of the monster eating Merrick ringing in my ears, propelling me forward.

That would be me. I would be next. *Run. Run run run.*

I forced myself to move faster, the trees and under-brush becoming shadowy blurs, my vision just as bad in the dark as a human's because I didn't have a wolf form yet. But I couldn't be more careful. I had to get as far away as possible before they noticed I was gone.

Just keep running. It doesn't matter where so long as it's away from that nightmare.

Branches caught on my dress and in my hair and whipped stinging slices against my bare arms and face. My toes caught on roots and bumps hidden in the darkness making me stumble, and rocks and branches sliced my bare feet. I bashed my shins against larger stones, rammed my hips and shoulders into tree trunks, but kept running.

I had to get farther, move faster. Go go go.

Sterling had let that thing eat his father alive.

My breath rushed in short, painful gasps.

Alive!

I jammed my foot on something, wrenched to the side to keep my balance, and slammed into a tree trunk. Pain shot through my face and the world spun and went black for a second.

Blindly, I staggered forward. I couldn't stop. Not for anything. But my foot hit empty air and I crashed forward, tumbling down a rocky incline and splashing into deep, freezing, rushing water.

The current wrenched me under and tossed me around and around. My body screamed for air, but I couldn't find the surface. My shoulder and the side of my head slammed into something hard, and sparks flashed across my vision before being consumed by writhing watery darkness.

I scraped against something else, broke the surface, somehow managed to gasp in a watery breath, but was shoved back under before I could even think to get my bearings and save myself.

I was moving too fast and my lungs screamed for air. I was going to drown and I was sure I hadn't gotten far enough away from that monster.

At least I wouldn't be alive when the thing ate me.

KNOX

I CRESTED THE RISE, MY FOUR LEGS CARRYING ME UP THE slope faster than my brothers on their two legs, and scanned the horizon. A dark red smear stained the eastern edge of the sky while the wind gusted, stronger on the hilltop than the valley below, and I could smell the moisture in the air.

A storm was fast on its way. A real one. Not like whatever had lit up the night just after midnight, jerking us from our sleep. From the color of this morning's sky and the ache in my right haunch — not to mention we were a month into the summer storm season — the coming storm would be bad, and we'd need to find cover soon.

Except I was pretty sure the real storm was the least of our worries, which was why Cyrus hadn't told us to turn around and head to the closest patrol shed to take cover.

Whatever had summoned that lightning had been powerful. After the first blinding flash and bone-rattling boom, a giant wave of power, that I'm sure had been felt all the way to Stonehaven, had crashed into us.

The wave had disappeared, and the night returned to quiet, but we couldn't risk thinking that because it had stopped everything was fine. Lightning didn't just come out of nowhere once then disappear. Not on a cloudless night. And it certainly didn't come with a wave of power.

The malicious god, Tzanagoth, was said to have fallen asleep in the heart of Anakar, the ruined temple complex in the center of the forest that lay before us, and while no gods had yet to wake from their magical slumber, we needed to confirm that this one hadn't finally broken the spell.

"Do you see anything?" Cyrus asked from halfway up the hill.

I raked my gaze over the thick forest beyond. The lightning had struck somewhere in the middle of those trees, but with them crowded close and the thick mist rolling and whirling between the trunks, I couldn't see anything in the predawn gray that might indicate what had happened, even with my excellent night vision. Which made me even more unsettled.

"I really hope it wasn't at the Anakar ruins," Bishop said, climbing to the top of the hill with Cyrus and stopping beside me. He reached down and brushed his fingers through my fur, trying to calm me with his touch even though I could sense his own worry through our twin bond.

I jerked away from him and loped down the hill.

I didn't need his touch to help calm me. I was fine. I wasn't even that upset.

So long as I was out in the open, preferably in my wolf form, I was fine, and I'd continue to be fine. I'd been fine for over a year.

But every time I got a little worried and it slipped through our bond, Bishop got concerned, like he was afraid my wolf was going to fully take over and I'd go feral again.

My wolf huffed at that. It hadn't really taken over, either. *So don't blame me.* Our fear had. That was the real beast inside me, the thing I battled with every day that I never admitted to anyone, not even my twin.

Very few in our pack had ever gone feral, and no one would have expected it from one of the alpha's sons. We were supposed to be the pack leaders, warriors at the front of the battle against the dangerous beasts roaming the land.

Of course, after Bishop had pulled me back to myself, everyone had *expected* I'd have a relapse. Even my brother. I was the strange one, the odd one, the one who didn't bother to smile for the sake of being polite. They said I liked the hunt too much, that I preferred my wolf form over my human one. I was already more wolf than man.

And they were right. My wolf didn't have to live up to expectations and didn't have to smile and be social when surrounded by too many people. I was free as a wolf in ways I'd never be free as a man, and I didn't give a fuck about my obligations as one of the alpha's sons. Just point me in the direction of a battle or hunt. That's all I wanted.

I found a break in the underbrush and a narrow game trail leading deeper into the trees and waited for Cyrus and Bishop to catch up. Mist curled over the ground, cold and thick, and the scent of forest decay and dirt sat heavy in the air, along with the teasing smell of a rabbit and some squirrels.

I ignored the urge to hunt down the rabbit and focused on smelling beyond the obvious forest scents for anything that might be dangerous.

We were almost done with our patrol of our borders and had already had to fight a small pack of grimalkins who thought one of our farmers and his livestock looked delicious. For all we knew, the rest of the grimalkins' pack had holed up here since the pack we'd fought had been smaller than usual and we didn't routinely patrol the Darkweald forest.

Not that they'd be smart enough to figure out that we ignored the forest since it was almost a day's march from the closest farmer and there were unwelcoming spirits in these mists. But without us patrolling the area, to their animal minds it might have seemed like a good place to call home.

I sniffed again. There was something just at the edge of my senses. A sweetness? A freshness? Something that didn't belong... or maybe it did. Maybe there were flowers in the heart of this murky forest. A god's power often influenced the area where he or she slept. Perhaps

Tzanagoth's magic had made it possible for something to bloom in the forest's perpetual twilight. Although given that Tzanagoth was a malicious god, I wouldn't have expected any flowers to bloom, especially ones that smelled sweet and fresh.

Smell anything? Cyrus asked in my head.

I pushed through the underbrush, stepping fully into the shadows and mist, and scented the air again. The sweet freshness grew a little stronger. It was definitely coming from somewhere to my left, but that didn't mean anything. I was supposed to be smelling for trouble while we headed straight to the ruins, and this didn't smell like trouble.

I'm scouting ahead.

Cyrus huffed his agreement, the communication more sensation than sound. He knew that if I didn't say there was trouble then there wasn't trouble.

I bounded down the trail a bit then slipped off the path into the underbrush, heading deeper into the forest to my right, away from the sweet scent. Cyrus and Bishop would stick to the path in their human forms while I'd search the surrounding area for signs of danger. Just because I couldn't smell something dangerous, didn't mean that something wasn't out there and hadn't left evidence behind.

The sweet fresh scent on my left continued to tease me despite purposely heading away from it, and my wolf started to double back toward it before I fully realized what we were doing.

I heaved myself back on track. Normally I'd just let him take over, especially since it was easier for him to be in control in our wolf form, but we couldn't lose ourselves in the hunt or even just curiosity right now. That lightning and power had announced the possibility of something seriously dangerous, and our brothers were depending on us to help keep them safe. As much as my wolf and I wanted to say fuck it to the world and all our obligations, we never wanted to endanger our brothers again.

This way, my wolf snarled, wrenching my head back toward the sweet scent. *Trouble.*

Something that smells good isn't trouble. Although I'd met more than a few females who'd smelled good and they'd certainly been trouble.

The wind gusted, swirling the mist and filling the air around with a hint of that sweet fresh scent and a big whiff of coppery tang. Blood. Lots of blood. Wolf shifter blood. And from the sweet freshness, female blood.

My wolf took off before I could come to the conclusion that it was necessary to check out what had happened.

A wolf shifter meant it was a pack member and everyone in the pack would want to know what had happened and who it was. Our pack wasn't small, but it wasn't too big that we didn't know or know of everyone in it, and someone had been seriously hurt.

KNOX

Pack has been hurt, my wolf growled to Cyrus and Bishop, racing faster as if he couldn't get to whoever it was quick enough. He must have recognized something about the scent that I hadn't, which was uncommon for everyone else but not for me. I spent days, sometimes months at a time in my wolf form, letting him control our body and wasn't completely aware of everything he did or everyone he encountered.

They could be dead, Cyrus replied grimly. He must have gotten a sniff of all that blood, too.

My wolf snarled at that and I crashed into a thorny bush, not caring that it scored my skin. The cuts weren't deep and even if I didn't shift, they'd heal soon enough.

I don't smell decay, Bishop replied quickly in an obvious attempt to calm my wolf.

Cyrus grunted at that. It could be too soon for decay to set in but he didn't want to say anything and risk setting me off. Now even he was walking on eggshells around me.

I shoved through the bush, my gaze instantly caught by a bit of white something, and jumped off the short steep edge of the riverbank into the mud.

The something white was a torn, filthy, bloody dress, on the broken body of a woman sprawled face down in the mud a few feet away. Scrapes and bruises covered her, and four deep wounds punctured her back as if she'd been stabbed with a wide, thick blade.

With the wind hissing through the trees and the rushing water, I couldn't hear from this distance if she was alive or not, but I couldn't see her breathing and I had a horrible feeling the injuries on her front would be worse.

I padded to her side, shifted, and gently rolled her over, my vision snapping to red, my anger roaring in my ears.

I was right. Her front was worse. Her face was one big bruise, her eyes swollen shut, her nose broken and still weeping blood, and the front of her dress had been ripped open, revealing four gashes, clearly claw marks, sliced across her chest.

Watery blood oozed from the wounds, pooling in the muddy puddle beneath her, and my anger blazed stronger. They hadn't just beaten her. They'd tortured her. Those slices weren't deep enough to kill right away and the sensitive flesh of both her breasts had been cut.

And the pack had thought *I* was a monster when I'd gone feral.

I'd never toyed with anyone like that, never tossed a person away in the river like they were garbage.

A growl bubbled in my throat. I didn't recognize her, not by her battered face or her matted, muddy blond hair, and neither I nor my wolf recognized her scent, but that didn't matter. I wasn't going to leave her here for the scavengers. She deserved to be taken back to pack land and given a proper burial.

And then I was going to hunt down whoever had done this to her and rip him to shreds.

My wolf heaved under my skin, determined to take over and start hunting now.

Just breathe, Knox, Bishop said, his voice in my head filled with worry. He wasn't even trying to hide his concern.

He and Cyrus pushed through the underbrush a few feet away from the thorny bush I'd gone through and staggered to a stop.

"We're going back to town," I snapped, picking up her limp, still slightly warm body, and cradling her against my chest. "We're going back now and burying—"

A gurgling gasp escaped her lips, followed by weak, ragged coughs, and water trickled from her mouth.

Fuck, she's alive? How the hell was she alive and I hadn't noticed? I was holding her in my arms. I should have heard her heartbeat.

But I was just so furious over what someone had done to her and — now that I was concentrating and up close — I heard that her pulse was slow and weak, barely there.

The eyelid on her least swollen eye fluttered and another gasping, weak cough, wracked her body.

"We have to get an elixir into her and get her back to town," Bishop said, hopping off the bank into the mud and reaching to take her from me as Cyrus opened his pack to get the precious ampul of healing elixir every patrol team carried in case of an emergency.

But before I could hand her over, another cough shook her, her eye cracked open, and her gaze locked on mine.

Heat and pressure erupted in my chest, roaring through me. My knees gave out and I dropped to the mud, clutching her, unable to look away.

Mine. She was mine. Every cell in my being knew she was mine—

No. I was hers. The power came from her. Somehow, without having said the vows and awakening the mating magic, she was binding our souls together.

The force tore into my essence, weaving through it and wrapping around it, growing tighter and tighter. She was trapping me. The cage of a soul bond was locking into place around my heart and if it solidified, I'd never be free.

No. Stop. I can't be trapped. I won't be trapped.

"Stop," I gasped.

She didn't respond, just kept staring at me... or

staring through me. I wasn't sure which. I wasn't even sure she was actually conscious.

Her breath stuttered and she whimpered, but I couldn't tell if it was from the magic or her injuries.

"Stop it," I growled. *Don't do this. Don't trap me.*

But the force of the magic surged, burning and hardening, tightening around my heart and soul until I couldn't breathe. Darkness crowded around me, crushing down, threatening my consciousness. I had to get free, had to stop this. Fight. Kill. Tear it all to shreds.

My wolf heaved and snarled, sensing my panic. It would protect me, protect her, protect what was mine—

No. We couldn't be bound together and I wouldn't be able to refuse the bond if my wolf took over. As much as it didn't want to be trapped, it somehow didn't see this mating as a cage like I did. It thought she was his and needed to protect her. Binding our souls was the first step in ensuring she was safe.

"Refute it with me." I shook her, desperate to wake her up. We could break the spell if we both refuted it before it took hold. If she knew that she was bonding to a complete stranger, she'd stop. She had to stop.

"Knox!" Bishop wrenched the woman from my arms, his eyes wide.

The distance stretched the magic between us, tearing at my soul, heaving me toward her, and Cyrus grabbed me around the waist and pulled me back.

The woman whimpered again and her eyelid slid shut, but that didn't sever the connection between us.

The magic had fully awakened, and now that she was unconscious, she wouldn't be able to refute me as her mate and end this. It was up to me and the force of my will alone.

"I refute you," I said, heaving against Cyrus's bear hug, my body still trying to get to her. "I refute you. I won't have you. You're not my mate!"

Ice exploded in my chest, tearing through the heat and pressure of the mating magic. It froze the magical cage around my heart and the chain binding me to this woman but didn't shatter it. I'd managed to cut off an active connection from my soul to hers, but I was still trapped, and even though we had yet to fully seal the bond, this stage was still permanent. I didn't know if there was any way to break it other than death.

CYRUS

WITH A FURIOUS ROAR, KNOX WRENCHED OUT OF MY GRIP and shifted, retreating into his wolf like he always did when his emotions were heightened.

"What just happened?" Bishop asked, as I cracked the wax seal on the ampul's stopper and dribbled the half ounce of elixir into her mouth. "Did she just mate bond with you?"

It sure looked like she had and from the look in Knox's eyes, he was pissed. I just wasn't sure if he was pissed that he'd been put in the position in the first place and forced to refute her or if he'd failed and was now stuck with a mate he didn't want.

Knox hopped onto the bank not acknowledging Bishop's remark and pushed through the bushes back to the trail.

"She was barely conscious," Bishop added, hurrying through the bushes after him. "I'm not even sure she knew who you were, and you didn't say your half of the vow. Do you even know her?"

Do you? You're familiar with a lot more females than I am, Knox said, his mental tone on *familiar* clear that he really meant fucked.

"No, I haven't slept with your mate before," Bishop shot back.

She's not my mate, Knox snarled.

Bishop glared at him. "I can feel the bond. You're blocking it, but it's there."

Guess he was pissed over not being able to break the mating magic before it took hold. Which was bad on so many levels.

Out of all of us, Knox was the worst one for the woman to have forced a bond on. He barely got along with others, shifters or otherwise, and he certainly wasn't interested in female attention. It was like Bishop, our youngest brother, had gotten all of the desire for social situations and flirting and had left Knox with nothing.

Except that wasn't really true. Knox hadn't been so closed off when we were children. At least not before the accident. He'd been a shy, somewhat reserved child, but he hadn't actively fled interacting with people, not like he did now, and I couldn't help but wonder if that distance he put between everyone except me and Bishop had been the reason for his fall into feral madness. There just weren't enough people he cared about to keep his primal nature at bay. One stress too many and without social support, our wolves took over to protect us.

And that was something I was going to have to keep an eye on. The stress of being forced into a mating he didn't want could be enough to tip him back into feralness.

So could losing that mate — whether he wanted her or not — and given the state of her injuries, I wasn't convinced that one ampul was going to be enough to save her.

"We need to get another ampul in her," I said. "We make for the patrol shed." Where we had one more dose of the healing elixir.

It was an hour out of our way if we wanted to go straight back to town, but I doubted she'd make it that far. I wasn't even sure she'd make it to the closest patrol shed. The healing elixirs worked wonders, but they weren't quick, and it took more than one — more than two actually — to bring someone back from the brink of death.

Except two was all we had access to. I could only hope it would be enough for her to hold on long enough to get back to town.

The wind gusted, swirling the mist and bringing with it the deep scent of rain. The storm that had been promised on the horizon had arrived and sooner than expected, making the shed an even better choice than heading straight to town.

I glanced back toward the heart of the forest. We still had no idea what had caused the lightning and power wave earlier this morning, and the longer we waited the greater the chance any clue as to what had happened would be washed away. But the woman was a priority. Even if she hadn't just soul bonded with Knox, saving her life was still a more immediate problem than investigating the lightning.

We hurried over the hill and into the valley on the other side. The clouds thickened, growing darker and darker and blotting out the sunrise. They released their promised downpour when we were only halfway to the shed. Stinging sheets of rain pelted us and wind gusts stole the breath from my lungs. But with no other obvious place to find shelter on the rolling grass and farmlands — and in need of that second ampul — all we could do was press forward as fast as we could.

We were drenched and shivering by the time we yanked open the shed door and hurried inside, Knox rushing in as well, surprising me.

He immediately shifted — thankfully resisting the urge to shake out his fur and spray everything in the tiny shed — and went to work starting the fire, leaving the woman to me and Bishop.

I grabbed the shed's only ampul of healing elixir from the hidden compartment by the door, cracked the seal, and dribbled it in her mouth. She looked even paler than when we'd first found her, and I was certain that wasn't just because the storm had washed away most of the mud and blood from her skin.

Blood still oozed from her deepest wounds and now her lips were blue. Even with the second ampul we still needed to warm her up and tend to her wounds, and I could only pray she hadn't lost too much blood and that two ampuls would be enough to save her.

I glanced at Knox, who was so focused on building the fire that it was painfully obvious he was trying not to look at the woman. I had no idea how to deal with this mess. If the bond had been set, they were going to have to seal it or there was a good chance they'd both go mad.

Except Knox was stubborn and would fight it. Probably to the point of irrevocable damage to both of them. How did I convince him to accept a mate he didn't want?

Hell, for all I knew she wouldn't want him, either.

Would they be able to break the magic if they both agreed? I'd never heard of anything like that happening once the bond had been formed, but then I'd never heard of anything like a bond forming without anyone saying the vows, either.

Knox had been adamant in refuting the bond. It should never have taken hold in the first place, and the magic remaining in the woman would have eventually faded. It wouldn't have been quick, usually months, but it would have gone away.

Except Bishop had said he'd felt Knox's mating bond, which meant it had progressed further than just one person starting the spell.

Did that mean this woman had intended to purposely trap Knox in a bond? We were the alpha's sons, and while it was expected my mate would join me in leading our pack there was precedent for the mate of a second or third son to become the female facet of the alpha unit. Of course, that was usually because that woman also took the first son as a mate as well, but there'd been that one rare female who hadn't mated both brothers.

Except I knew every eligible female in our pack and didn't recognize her. She didn't even smell like any of the other pack members. And if she'd really wanted to ensnare one of us with the goal of becoming a part of our pack's leadership, it would have been easier to trap Bishop. He wasn't wary of women like Knox was.

That and unless it had backfired on her, I doubted her plan was to be found almost dead in a river, hours away from our patrol route. She'd have had no way of guaranteeing that we'd even go into Darkweald... unless she was responsible for the lightning and the power.

Except given how weak her shifter essence was, indicating that she was almost powerless, it was even harder to believe she'd been responsible for last night's wave of power than her planning to trap Knox in a bond.

No. Whatever had happened to her and however she'd managed to mate with Knox, it hadn't been planned.

And that only meant I needed to stop trying to figure everything out right this second and focus on saving the woman.

CYRUS

I STRIPPED OUT OF MY WET CLOTHES AND TOOK HER FROM Bishop.

"I'll get some fresh water," Bishop said, but Knox pushed past him, reaching for the bucket by the door before Bishop could grab it.

"I'll go," Knox growled not bothering to look at us, and he march back out into the storm.

"We're not going to be able to convince him to hold her to warm her up," Bishop said as he stripped out of his wet clothes as well and opened one of the many water-proof trunks at the back of the small room.

I laid the woman on the floor by the hearth as close to the fire Knox had started as was safe and sliced open the rest of her dress with a claw. "You honestly thought we might? I doubt we'd be able to convince him to do it even if we were in a room ten times this size."

"We both know he's not an asshole. I thought he'd be

concerned enough to use their bond to help comfort her," Bishop replied, pulling on a dry pair of pants then grabbing another pair for me along with the pack with our non-magical healing supplies. "If she wakes, she'll be in pain and probably confused. The bond is new, but his presence will still help keep her calm."

The door flew open, and Knox stormed in with a bucket filled with water from the well. His gaze instantly locked on the woman, her battered body now fully exposed, the scrapes and bruises and bleeding gashes on her chest bright against her pale skin.

His eyes, which were almost perpetually dark with his wolf not the brown with green flecks he'd been born with, narrowed and the muscles in his jaw tightened. "I'll keep watch." He set the bucket beside me and stormed back outside.

Yeah, wishful thinking to hope he'd want to hold her. He wasn't purposely cruel, but this went so far beyond what he was comfortable with, I wouldn't be surprised if he stayed in his wolf form for days.

"Let's get her wounds cleaned and dressed. With luck the clothes in his pack aren't too wet and they'll dry before she wakes. We can at least give her his scent."

We used up all our clean gauze and linen packing the stab wounds and gashes on her front and the stab wounds on her back and then binding it down with strips wrapped around her chest. Bishop set down a blanket, laid down, and, mindful of her injuries, drew her close, his bare chest to her mostly bare back in the hopes that any flesh-to-flesh contact from him and not just her mate would help her. In the very least, his body — along with a second blanket that I set over both of them — would help warm her.

I pulled Knox's damp, but thankfully not drenched, shirt from the bottom of his travel pack and set it on the floor by the fire to dry then dug through the supply trunks for rations. We hadn't eaten breakfast, choosing to chase after whatever had brought the lightning, and if we were going to have to wait out the storm, we might as well eat something.

The trunks were maintained on a seasonal basis, kept fully stocked for those rare occasions, like now, when a patrol didn't have time to hunt and needed shelter. Something I was grateful for since there was no way of telling how long the storm would last. It could be a few hours or, if it had originated over the lands where a few of the storm gods slept, it could be days and we'd need the dried food supplies for our meals.

For the woman's sake, I hoped it blew over quickly. I could still barely hear her pulse even with two ampuls of elixir in her, and while it took time for the elixir to work, the fact that she hadn't responded yet wasn't good.

Giving her a third one would have better increased her chances of survival. Except we didn't have a third one. And if we did and it was already too late for her then I'd just be throwing away valuable elixir.

I found a bag of dried oats and set them simmering in a pot of water over the fire then sat by Bishop and the woman to mind our meal and monitor the dryness of Knox's shirt. I didn't know how Knox would react to Bishop holding his mate while she was naked and injured, and while flesh to flesh contact might be better for her, it would be safer for Bishop if she were dressed.

Being possessive wasn't common for our pack, not like some of the other shifter species and packs, but it wasn't completely unheard of, either. Even if Knox didn't have the possessive trait, it was still common for newly mated males to be overprotective of their females, and just looking at this woman made all my protective instincts rise up and howl. And I wasn't soul bonded to her.

"Where do you think she came from?" Bishop asked his voice low, barely carrying over the storm howling outside.

"I don't know." I brushed a dark blond strand of wet hair away from her swollen and purple cheek. Shining sisters, it hurt just looking at her. "Even if she didn't come from one of the other packs, I doubt she'd have come from the north. There isn't a town within a five day's journey from the north side of Darkweald, if there's a town out there at all."

And she certainly wouldn't have been alone. She'd have been with at least a dozen others regardless of where she'd come from. Even if she'd come by sea — the safest way to reach pack lands — and landed in Savaria, the port city four days west from our town, she still wouldn't have been traveling alone.

As much as we and the other sentient races had spent generations trying to tame these lands, the power seeping from the sleeping gods was too strong. The beast and spirit population never diminished, it could only be kept back, and that meant traveling between civilized lands was dangerous even for a group of armed warriors.

"Whatever her situation, it can't be good," I mused. "Spirits don't usually do this kind of damage and a beast would have finished her off and eaten her."

"Unless she managed to escape and got swept down river," Bishop suggested, but he didn't sound as if he believed that.

A lot of her scratches and bruises could be explained by her fleeing through the forest and being tossed down a rushing river, but the puncture marks in her back and front and the claw cuts across her breasts without any other mauling injuries suggested it hadn't been a beast. She would have had more claw and teeth marks on her arms. People almost always raised their arms to defend themselves and beasts always slashed and bit those easy targets.

"That still doesn't explain why she was in Darkweald in the first place," I said. "She has no power, she's barely a wolf, and I doubt she'll have much more when she recovers."

If she recovers, a worried little voice whispered to me.

And if that happened, there was a chance we'd lose Knox to his wolf again. Permanently this time.

BISHOP

Cyrus growled — I wasn't sure he was fully aware he was doing it — and leaned forward to stir our breakfast. I couldn't sense his emotions like I could Knox's, but I knew him well enough to know the growl wasn't anger but fear. It had barely been a year since Knox had come back to us, and this woman threatened to shatter what little hold he'd managed to regain of his humanity.

In the blink of an eye, she'd mate bonded with him, and I still had no idea how she'd done it or why.

Unlike the mythical angels, our mate bond was more symbolic than symbiotic. Yes, a bond was formed with magic from our soul and that could increase an emotional connection between mates — or in the case of me and Knox, between twins — but she couldn't draw strength or power from him like an angelic bond, so bonding with him couldn't have been a desperate attempt to live.

She whimpered, making my pulse trip. Waking up was a sign the elixir was working, but given her injuries that probably wasn't the best for her. She was going to be in pain and there wasn't anything we were able to do about it.

The patrol sheds weren't stocked with sleeping elixirs since those were even more precious than healing ones and there was always a chance a beast or a thief would come by the sheds and find the hidden compartment and steal it. And even though there'd been extensive studies, no one had found a non-magical sedative or painkiller that worked on shifters. Warriors on patrol we're expected to just tough it out if they were so badly injured that they needed both the team's and the shed's elixirs. No one thought we'd need to tend to a female barely clinging to life and that it would be better if she remained unconscious while she healed.

I brushed my hand over her damp hair, trying to calm her. We couldn't afford for her to fully wake and panic over being surrounded by strange men. She could hurt herself worse than she already was. But it would have been better if it was Knox holding her. Even if her human mind didn't recognize him, her wolf would, and that might be enough to help her.

Except even with his reinforced mental barrier hard and cold between us, I could still feel his emotions seeping through: rage, frustration, confusion, and on top of all that fear.

His fear was so strong it twisted in my chest, making

me afraid. I didn't know if my fear was just because of his, or if I was also afraid he'd retreat fully into himself and let his wolf take over again, or worse, lock his wolf down and do the only thing that we knew would fully sever the mating bond before it got too strong: kill her.

I tightened my grip on the woman and curled more protectively around her, unable to help myself.

I couldn't believe she'd meant to bond with him. I wasn't even sure she'd been conscious, so there was no way for her to know who she was bonding with, if she'd even been aware that she was bonding with someone in the first place. This wasn't her fault and I wouldn't let Knox take his fear out on her. If her mate couldn't be trusted to protect her, I would.

And with the way things were, it was going to be up to me. Cyrus was obligated to protect the pack, and he wouldn't hesitate to imprison or kill her if he thought she was a threat.

Cyrus got up, grabbed a small pot of honey along with bowls and spoons for three from the trunks, then checked Knox's shirt.

"This is dry and the oatmeal is almost ready," he said, no indication in his voice that he thought the woman was dangerous. "Let's get her dressed so she's not completely naked when Knox comes in for breakfast."

Now it was my turn to huff at him for making a ridiculous statement. "You honestly think he'll come in and eat?" Sure, lying with her was a lot more involved than sitting in the same room with her, but he'd still made a point to sit outside when we all knew no one and nothing would be out in the storm and there was no point in keeping watch.

"I'll make him," Cyrus said, his wolf rising to the surface and darkening his eyes. "Now prop her up so we can get his shirt over her head."

She wasn't very big, so it was easy to support her head and sit up at the same time. She whimpered, her breath turning sharp with pain, but thankfully didn't wake, and with the two of us, we easily pulled on Knox's shirt, which was practically a dress on her — an extremely short dress, but still a dress — then settled her back on the floor.

I set the blanket back over her but didn't lie beside her so I could eat. With another soft whimper, she curled in on herself and pulled Knox's shirt up to her nose. Her breath evened out and frustration twisted in my chest.

Her reaction to his scent, even while unconscious, was proof she needed him and hard proof that she and Knox had indeed mate bonded. Knox should be here with her.

The muscles in Cyrus's jaw flexed at that, as if he'd needed proof and not just my word about the bond, then pulled his attention away and spooned out three helpings of oatmeal.

Breakfast is ready, he called out, speaking in both my mind and Knox's.

I'll catch something on the way home, Knox growled back, including me because Cyrus had.

We'll be hampered by the woman. I don't want you hunting, Cyrus insisted.

I'll make it home without eating then. If it hadn't been obvious before, it was clear now, Knox was avoiding the woman. He could usually handle an hour, let alone a quick meal, in the shed before he became too uncomfortable in the small space.

We don't know when the storm will end. We need to eat and we need to talk, Cyrus growled a hint of his power slipping through the link. *You can go back outside when we're done.*

We can talk just fine right now, Knox huffed.

No. Cyrus's eyes flashed to full black and his canines extended, his wolf threatening to take over. *You'll eat and you'll eat now!*

His power raced through the mental link, flooding both Knox and me — since the only way Cyrus could command someone as powerful as Knox was to not hold back — and I scooped a mouthful of bland, boiled oats into my mouth before I had a chance to sweeten it with the honey.

Knox whined on the other side of the door, being a stubborn asshole and fighting the command.

Now! Cyrus barked, sending another wave of his power crashing over us.

The woman cried out, Cyrus's power affecting her

even while unconscious and not directly connected to our mental link, and the shed door flew open as if her pain and not Cyrus's command had been what had compelled him to come in.

BISHOP

Knox stood in the doorway in his human form, water dripping from his hair and down his naked body into a puddle at his feet. His gaze locked on the woman and for a second his expression was ragged and filled with desperate heartbreak before vanishing behind a mask of anger.

"You're a fucking asshole," he snarled, his fear picking up and his eyes jumping over the walls of the small shed.

"And we need to eat and talk about what we're going to do with the woman." Cyrus gave a pointed look at the third bowl of oatmeal by his knee.

Knox trembled for a moment, still fighting Cyrus's command, then dropped to the floor beside me and picked up his breakfast.

"We're not going to do anything." Knox shoveled a large spoonful into his mouth and dutifully chewed and swallowed, glaring at Cyrus the whole time. "The second we get home, I'm going to ask Whil if she can break the bond."

"The bond is already set." I could feel it even through the mental shield he'd put up preventing me from fully connecting with him with our twin bond. He'd frozen the mating bond — not just blocked it like our bond — cutting himself off from the woman as fully as he could. But it didn't matter what he did, he couldn't sever it.

Cyrus frowned. "Do you think Whil can break it?"

"She's a sorcerer. She's figured out how to take the water leaking from Airmed's resting place and turn it into a healing elixir. If she can't break the bond outright, then some god has empowered water or sap or a flower or something that can." Knox's gaze flickered to the woman and he angrily ate another spoonful of bland oatmeal. "I don't care how long it takes. I won't be trapped in a bond."

It sounded like he'd spent more than just the short time he'd been outside thinking about this. Had he thought about asking Whil to break our twin bond?

My wolf snarled at that. Knox was ours. Just like our mate would be — and I wasn't going to think about the fact that we'd always thought Knox and I would share a mate because of that.

We shared a bond very few did, and my wolf and I would fight with everything we had to keep it. We were two halves of the same soul, more than just brothers. We wouldn't allow him to force the pain and emptiness of a broken bond onto us, and we didn't want him to force that on the woman, either. She was in enough pain already.

"Breaking the bond will hurt both of you," I pointed out, even though it didn't need pointing out. Everyone knew breaking a bond — which as far as we knew could only be done through death — was devastating for the surviving member. And that was why not everyone spoke the vows to awaken the magic for a mating bond. Not because they didn't love their mate, but because our world was dangerous and warriors often didn't want their mates to suffer if something happened to them.

"I won't be trapped," Knox insisted as if that explained everything. And perhaps it did. He'd been trapped in the dark in that cave-in for days when we were kids and he'd never been the same since. The hint of panic I felt through our muted bond was the same panic he felt surrounded by too many people, in a crowded room or, hell, even just spending too much time in a small room. To him they were the same as being trapped under all that rubble.

Still— "She should have a say in the matter, too." It wasn't just him who was going to suffer the effects of their broken bond.

"No," Cyrus said, shocking me. "Knox tried to refute her. He has every right to break the bond whether it hurts her or not. He shouldn't have to be stuck with a mate he doesn't want."

Well, when put that way...

"No one should be stuck in a loveless mating." Cyrus's

gaze drifted to the woman and his wolf rose to the surface, but I couldn't tell if it was anger at the situation with Knox or his situation and the possibility that, as the oldest, he was going to have to mate with someone he didn't really love for the sake of the pack. "Besides, we don't know anything about this woman. She could be cruel and selfish. She's weak, maybe she ended up almost dead in Darkweald because she was trying to become more powerful in an unnatural way."

"You think she had something to do with the lightning?" Knox asked, his attention locked on his meal, his fear starting to seep stronger through our connection even though he'd only been in the shed for a handful of minutes.

"I first thought no, but trying to get Tzanagoth's power would explain why she was in the forest." Cyrus sighed and pushed a damp lock of hair that had come loose from his braid out of his eyes. "We won't know until she wakes and we have no idea when that will be."

"Even then," Knox growled, finishing his meal and storming back to the door. "I don't care if she's a goddess of absolute goodness. I'm breaking our bond."

KNOX

I couldn't get home to Whil fast enough. It felt like forever before the storm passed when really it had blown through quickly and only took up the morning. But then we moved at an agonizingly slow pace, trying to balance speed with not aggravating the woman's injuries and worsening her condition.

The woman. My mate.

There just was so much wrong with those two words.

A mate meant someone living with me, around me, crowding me. Just the thought made my pulse race. It was difficult enough to be around my brothers and they understood me. This woman, like everyone else, wouldn't.

And it didn't matter that my soul and my wolf were certain that wouldn't be the case, that she, even if she wasn't as broken as I was, would still accept me. That was just the mating bond.

It was already hard to ignore her, to resist the need to gather her in my arms and comfort and protect her, and that desire to be near her, to do more with her and seal the bond, would only get stronger the longer the situation went on.

As it was, I'd only managed to hold myself back because Cyrus had commanded me to eat and the shed's fifteen by fifteen windowless space had made me feel — a lot more than usual — like I was suffocating.

It had been easier to ignore the frozen bond in my chest once I was outside, but not by much. There had only been a door and a few feet between us, and my wolf really wanted to shove Bishop aside and take his place beside her. It was certain with her in our arms, the small space wouldn't bother us so much.

I wasn't convinced. Nothing alleviated the anxiety of feeling trapped except getting outside. Outside was the only place I was truly safe.

Except now we were outside, the gloom of twilight heavy around us, and there was no door separating us. I tried to roam ahead, but even if Cyrus hadn't cared how far I went, I couldn't get very far. The chain around my heart that I was determined to keep frozen kept yanking me back, drawing all my senses to her.

I'd heard that the compulsion from the mating bond to be with your mate in every way, especially when it first formed, was powerful, but this went beyond powerful. It was consuming. She needed me, needed to be protected and held and loved. It didn't matter that I didn't even know her name. She was mine and there wasn't anything I wouldn't do for her.

Which wasn't true. It was gods damned not true.

I only felt that way because of the magic connecting us. It wasn't a real emotion. It couldn't be, so I concentrated on wrapping more mental ice into the cage around my heart and the chain linking us together.

She whimpered and my wolf snarled. Bishop needed to be more careful. She would be better off with me carrying her.

Fuck, no. I wrenched my attention back to the rolling grass-covered foothills and the shadow of the towering mountain in front of us and the faint glimmer of light at the mountain's base. Home.

Focus on home and getting to Whil and getting free. The woman was just fine with Bishop. Given her injuries, she would have been whimpering and moaning just lying in the shed. Besides, her pain, while regrettable, didn't matter.

I didn't care.

I couldn't care. Not if I wanted to get through severing our mating bond as unscathed as possible.

This ordeal would be over soon. I just had to hold on a little longer and keep the ice around my heart strong. I sure as hell couldn't give in and hold her. Holding her would lead to other things. Nothing serious because she was too badly injured, but some gentle kisses wouldn't be a prob—

Stop it! No holding. No kissing. No nothing with this stranger.

Why couldn't I remember she was a complete stranger?

For all I knew Cyrus was right and she'd been trying to strengthen her pathetically weak essence by waking Tzanagoth.

It was full dark by the time we reached Stonehaven, the pack's town that sprawled down the mountain's sloping base. The original buildings at the top — Old Town — were almost a thousand years old, although thankfully they'd been modernized over the years. They were big and blocky, and with the exception of the alpha's residence, which was surrounded by gardens, were crowded together with a mix of shops and residences interspersed with a warren of gardens and small parks all surrounded by the original town wall.

Over the years, though, the pack had grown beyond the couple hundred that Old Town could hold and with the area surrounding our land becoming safer, houses and shops had been built beyond the wall, the architecture growing more modern the closer you got to the edge of town.

Much to my surprise, Lucius, Zavier, and Whil waited on the outskirts of town with two travel packs resting on the ground by their feet.

Lucius, our first beta and primary advisor since he'd retired from being huntmaster — and was really better suited to administration than battling beasts — along with Zavier, his nephew and newly made warrior who showed great promise, were dressed to travel.

"What's wrong?" Cyrus asked the second we were in earshot. We'd arrived later than scheduled, but given the strange lightning, a late arrival would have been expected. Zavier might have been sent to greet us to find out if we needed anything immediately, but Lucius and Whil would have stayed in the Residence. And no one would have brought travel packs with them or worn the protective leathers necessary to travel the mountain pass to Savaria and the lands beyond.

"Jundar called an emergency meeting of the Mountain and Sea Alliance to discuss the increase in beast activity in the area," Lucius said, his attention on my mate.

My wolf curled his lips back, but I managed to swallow his growl before we released it.

She was *not* my mate. She was just a woman. I didn't want her. Anyone could look at her and it didn't matter, and while I wouldn't be able to stop Cyrus from telling everyone I was mate bonded to her, I'd hoped he'd spare me the attention and keep it between us and Whil.

And if I really wanted that, I couldn't afford to get all protective and reveal the situation on my own.

Except no matter what I did, my focus always returned to her. I'd yank it away, be determined not to pay any attention to her, and be unable to resist seconds later.

"We need to head out," the older man said, "but we

wanted to wait until you got back before we left. I'm assuming you investigated that lightning and power wave?"

"We didn't get a chance," Cyrus said, his expression dark.

Yeah, strange lightning and power, and now the towns on the other side of the mountain were experiencing the same increase in beast activity we were. Not good.

"We found her in Darkweald barely alive," Bishop added. "Two ampuls of healing elixir this morning and she's still unconscious."

"What happened to her?" Zavier asked, drawing closer to get a better look and making my pulse pick up. He was young but of an age where he was courting potential mates—

I shook my head, trying to clear it.

He wasn't going to flirt with my mate. She was unconscious and she wasn't my gods dammed mate!

Bishop tightened his hold on her, drawing her closer to his chest as if he, too, instinctually wanted to protect her, and even that made my wolf heave within me.

We should be holding her, protecting her.

Jeez. How many times was I going to have to tell myself we wanted nothing to do with her? We didn't even know her.

"We don't know what happened," Bishop replied.

"We'll send a hunt team out in the morning to restock shed twelve and see if there's anything in Darkweald to indicate what happened," Cyrus said. "Unless you know what happened," he added, turning his attention to Whil.

The willowy fae with her ever-so-slightly glowing skin pulled her bright green gaze up from the woman.

Damn it! Was everyone going to stare at her? Did Whil know about the mating bond?

I mentally rolled my eyes at myself. Of course she knew. She could sense bonds and magic and all manner of things shifters couldn't. She'd have known I was chained to the woman before Lucius and Zavier had even spotted us on the road.

"I have a few theories," she replied, thankfully not mentioning my unexpected mating bond with a stranger. "But nothing concrete."

"Anything we need to deal with immediately?" Bishop asked, his worry over the situation seeping into me even though I was actively trying to keep him out.

"Probably, but until we know more, there's nothing we can do." She frowned, and her gaze drifted to the rolling hills beyond the town that were cloaked in darkness and thankfully not back to the woman.

"And with that, I should get going." Lucius nodded at Zavier who started to race back into town.

"Wait," Cyrus said, and a shiver of his power rushed over us even though I knew he wasn't purposely trying to command us. "You better be taking at least half a squad."

"I might be retired, but I'm not an idiot," Lucius huffed, and Cyrus jerked his chin at Zavier, giving him permission to continue on his errand. "If Jundar is concerned, then the pass isn't safe even in the daytime."

Which meant our situation was worse than we'd first thought. Beasts in the pass meant they were getting closer and closer to our town, and if they were also encroaching on the borders of Ciliaran and the other towns, states, and kingdoms in the Alliance then that meant for some reason there'd been an increase in their population and that would endanger the lives of all our farmers as well as trade among our communities.

I had a bad feeling that something dangerous was on its way, and I could tell from everyone's expression that they feared the same thing as well.

And if something dangerous — or rather something more dangerous than usual — was coming our way, I couldn't afford to be distracted by this bond. It was getting harder and harder to focus on the conversation between Cyrus and Lucius. It'd be even harder in the middle of a battle.

Lucius's attention flickered back to the woman. "I hope rescuing one life doesn't endanger everyone else's."

The asshole! My wolf seized control of our body, sent a wave of our power over all the shifters in the group, demanding submission, and snapped at Lucius, not caring that we were raising suspicions. Lucius dropped to one knee, his eyes wide at the sudden use of force, while both Cyrus and Bishop staggered.

KNOX

"Enough," Cyrus barked, his own power tearing mine apart and forcing me to bow my head in submission to him. "We weren't going to leave her for dead. I'm going to assume Jundar will ask for more warriors. Tell him we want more healing water for Whil to refine in exchange."

"Yes, alpha," Lucius said, still kneeling.

"Good. Now—" Cyrus turned to Whil who, because she wasn't a shifter, hadn't been affected by my or Cyrus's power. "Walk with us. We need to talk."

Without waiting for her response, he strode down the main street toward the center of New Town.

She quirked a sculpted golden eyebrow, her attention sliding to me then the woman — Oh yeah, she knew the truth — then rushed to fall into step beside him.

Bishop hurried to walk on Cyrus's other side, and I pushed ahead, trying to get them to hurry up. The sooner we dealt with the bond, the sooner I'd be free. But the urge to stay by the woman's side, to shift, to take her from my brother churned inside me, and I kept slowing, drawn to her whether I wanted to be or not.

"You should probably be talking with Nova instead of me. She's the party planner," Whil snickered once we were out of earshot from Lucius. "It can be a surprise party for the rest of the pack." She burst out laughing. "I don't think anyone bet that you'd be the first of the alpha's sons to mate."

This isn't funny, I snarled as we reached the main square in New Town and took the lead, bounding up a narrow side street with shallow steps leading up to the Old Town wall. The last thing I wanted was to march past the dozen pubs and restaurants lining Main Street while having this conversation. Even if only my brothers and Whil could hear my side of the conversation, people could figure out the truth from Whil's responses. *I don't want a party. I want it broken.*

"You what?" Whil missed the first step and stumbled up the next three.

Cyrus grabbed her arm before she fell, helping her right herself. "Is that something you can do?"

"Why would you make the bond if you don't want it?" she asked.

Because I didn't make it. I rushed up the stairs and around the corner, but my wolf jerked me to a stop and the frozen chain in my chest strained to draw me back to her. We couldn't see her anymore, we needed to go back.

No. We could wait. Bishop would catch up soon enough.

But damn it. We didn't want to wait on anything. She was ours and we needed to seal the bond and properly claim her.

For the love of—!

There was no way in hell we were claiming her. Even if we wanted to, she was in no condition to have sex.

Which, jeez, wasn't the point.

Bishop, with his precious, unwanted cargo, rounded the corner and the pressure in my chest eased.

"We don't know what happened," he said. "We found her near death and when Knox picked her up, she initiated the mating bond. I don't even think she was conscious."

"I didn't think it was possible to initiate that kind of bond while unconscious." Whil laid a hand on the woman's forehead. "At least certainly not for shifters."

"But it is for other races?" Cyrus asked.

"Angels have no control over their mating bonds. No words, no conscious thought. It could be with a complete stranger they've never met, and they could be barely alive, and the bond would still form," Whil explained as we rounded another corner and reached the road that followed the Old Town wall around the original town. "But she's clearly not an angel."

"Are we sure?" Cyrus asked. "Her essence says she's one of us, but it's weak. Could she be a half-breed?"

"Not with an angel," Whil said. "Even if the portals to

this realm were unlocked and the beings from the Realm of Celestial Light decided to pay us a visit, angels can only procreate with other angels. There are no half-breeds. And even if one of her parents was something else, you're either born a shifter or you're not. There's no in between."

I don't care what she is, I snapped as we reached the main gate to Old Town and hurried up the road to our home. *I only care that this fucking bond is broken.*

"Watch your tone," Cyrus growled in warning, his power rolling off him. Whil was a revered member of our community and had been so for almost a thousand years — despite the fact that she still looked about thirty. With her ability to weave raw magical energy into spells, she could have easily taken over the pack at any time, but instead, chose to just be a councilor, offering her wisdom and abilities when asked.

My wolf whined at Cyrus's power and the woman whimpered, sending more churning desperate need twisting inside me.

Bishop's worry increased as well, and for a second all the emotions and need were too much. The road was too narrow, the walls of the buildings on either side of me too high. I needed space. I had to get out of there, but the bond wouldn't let me leave her side. I was going to suffocate from the pressure.

"We have to do something," Bishop said.

We reached the courtyard in front of our residence, the grand, three-story fortress only visible against the shadow of the mountain because of the lights at the main doors and in a dozen of the windows. Home. Except the thought of going inside made my chest tight. I had to stay out here, regain my mental equilibrium. And somehow, my wolf actually agreed with me.

Except if Whil could break the bond right away—

"I don't know if it's possible to break the bond. I need to do some reading," Whil mused, shattering what little hope I had that this mess would be fixed immediately. "I also need to talk to her..." She drew the word out as if expecting one of us to give her a name. When we didn't supply her with one, she shrugged. "She might have a clue about what happened. If she wasn't conscious during the bonding, then maybe there was something else going on and it isn't a true bond. It might not be as permanent as it looks."

"You mean there might be a way to break it?" Bishop asked.

"If it's a false mating bond, maybe," Whil said, "but I'll need more information."

"I want to talk to her first," Cyrus said, pulling open the front door and holding it for Whil. "We don't know if she's dangerous. For all we know she's connected to that wave of power."

Whil's expression turned grim. "That's something else I need to think about."

Figure out how to break the bond first, I said, managing to stay outside despite the pressure closing in around me.

I didn't care how important that lightning and power

were, I was losing my mind. There was too much pressure from too many things, and I was going to lose control over one of them. I didn't want to risk that one thing being my need to resist the compulsion to seal the bond. Sealing it gave it strength and then all possibility of breaking it would be lost whether it was a fake bond or not.

AUDREY

I TOSSED THIS WAY AND THAT ON A DARK OCEAN OF AGONY, my whole body on fire. Sharp pain sliced through my face and chest while throbbing pain radiated through the rest of me. I tried to open my eyes, but couldn't, wasn't even sure if I could turn thought into action, and was dragged deeper into the painful darkness.

A moment later — or was that an eternity? — I bobbed back up to the surface. Voices murmured around me and the agony in my body burned stronger. I strained again to open my eyes. I couldn't just lie there. That monster was after me. It might have eaten Merrick, but that didn't mean I was off the menu. But the painful darkness dragged me back under again.

Another eternal moment and a wave of power threatened to crush me. I hadn't even clawed my way back to the surface. Sterling had to be furious to radiate everything he had and pound into my subconscious like that, which meant I was in danger. I *had* to wake up.

Wake up. Open your eyes. Run.

But the more I struggled, the deeper the darkness dragged me down. The pain and fear and knowledge that I'd been so stupid was too much. Better to curl into the darkness and hide from everything. At least in the darkness I wasn't weak, wasn't so pathetic that my life was considered worthless by my pack.

A trickle of cold seeped into the darkness.

I was so pathetic my fated mate didn't even want me.

The cold grew, pushing the pain to the edge of my senses. But instead of something flooding into the hole carved inside me, the cold just kept pushing, making the hole bigger and bigger, leaving me frozen and achingly hollow.

Of course my fated mate wouldn't want me. I was a shifter who couldn't shift. I was so weak my wolf nature refused to wake or even acknowledge me. Who wanted to be stuck with someone like that for the rest of his life? No one. I wasn't good for anything. Sterling had been telling me I was useless from the moment I moved into his house, and Royce had said the same when he'd refuted our fated mate bond.

Except the fated mating call hadn't been real. Royce and Sterling had used magic to manipulate me.

But that thought only made my insides twist with shame. I should have known fate would never bond me with someone as powerful as Royce, and I certainly should have known that even if by some miracle the fated mating call had been real, Royce would never have accepted me.

And now I had who-knew-how-many months suffering this painful, hollow ache of the incomplete bond until it went away.

Except a part of me feared it wouldn't go away.

It felt too powerful. A frozen emptiness that threatened to completely hollow me out into a lifeless shell. It felt locked within my cells, imprinted in my soul, a permanent reminder of how foolish I'd been.

To think I could be loved, be free, be anything other than myself.

I was weak *and* stupid and the only reason I was alive was because I'd gotten lucky and Merrick had stumbled across Sterling's ritual before that monster could eat me.

Oh, God. That monster!

I woke with a start, my pulse pounding along with my head... and my face... my whole body, really. I was one enormous aching bruise. But strangely not much more than that when, given the injuries I'd had when I'd raced blindly into the forest, I should have been in agony.

The icy hollowness, however, was stronger than before, threatening to overwhelm me, so perhaps I was just too numb and heartbroken to notice how much pain I was in.

The rich scent of wood smoke and something else, something deeply masculine, hung in the air, wrapping around my senses, and while I had a strange feeling it should be comforting me, it couldn't penetrate the icy emptiness consuming me.

I dragged my senses away from the scent and opened my eyes. I lay on my side, covered with a soft blanket, facing a plain white wall and a simple, large window. Outside I could see sunlight streaming through a large leafy tree branch and beyond that brilliant blue sky.

None of which gave me any clue as to where I was. I wasn't in my room or anywhere in Merrick's house — or rather Sterling's house now that he'd murdered his father — since the window frame didn't match any I was familiar with.

Something creaked behind me and my pulse leaped into a rapid beat again. I wasn't alone. Wherever I was, someone was watching me.

Please don't let it be Royce or Sterling... or that monster. I didn't know why they'd have kept me alive and in a bed, when they'd tried to serve me up to that thing last night. I would have expected them to lock me in a damp basement to await whatever they planned. But being comfortable in a bed could easily be another way to torture me before putting me back on the menu.

I glanced over my shoulder. A large, intimidating, beautiful man sat in a chair between me and the door, watching me with moss green eyes. His expression was hard but that only seemed to accentuate his rugged, masculine beauty.

His shoulders were easily twice as broad as mine and his biceps probably the size of my thighs. Without a doubt he was a foot to a foot and a half taller than me, and I was about average height for a woman. His brown hair had been shaved at the sides but left long on top and twisted into a thick braid that reached the nape of his neck, making him look like a Medieval warrior. Add to that at least a day's worth of scruff on his square jaw along with the enormous feral energy radiating from him, and it was obvious he was a powerful, dangerous wolf shifter.

Relief flickered through me, but the feeling barely burst to life before being consumed with fear. Just because I didn't know this man, didn't mean I wasn't still at Sterling and Royce's mercy. This man could be a mercenary hired to keep the pack in line now that Merrick was dead, or worse, to keep *me* in line until it was time to sacrifice me.

AUDREY

"I'm not going to hurt you," the man said, his voice soft but still gruff as if he wasn't quite sure how to deal with me, which didn't fit with him being Sterling's hired muscle. "What's your name?"

That really didn't fit with being hired muscle. Even if Sterling hadn't bothered to mention my name, the kind of guy he'd hire to watch me wouldn't care. That and why hire someone when there were more than enough members of the pack who'd happily guard me then hand me over to a monster?

I should have thought of that from the start. If Sterling was now the alpha, his father's betas would need to prove themselves to keep their position in the pack, and while I'd thought most of them were okay men, I didn't really know them well and wasn't sure how far they'd go to keep their position in the pack.

But if that was the case, did that mean I'd managed to escape? Was I actually free?

The icy hollowness swelled, overwhelming me for a second. Even if sacrificing Merrick to the monster had gotten Sterling whatever he wanted, if I ever showed my face anywhere near pack lands, Sterling would go after me. He'd probably have someone keeping an eye on Mila in her new pack just to see if I'd go to her.

If I had, in fact, managed to escape my old life, I had to make a clean cut. I couldn't reach out to Mila in any way, and I had to figure out how to get as far away from pack lands as possible — and I doubted that wherever I was, was far enough.

I needed to figure out how to get out of the country— hell, go to Europe or Asia if I could find the money. It didn't matter that my wolf hadn't woken and I still looked like an easy target for any super looking to cause trouble. I would fight with everything I had to keep the freedom I'd somehow managed to achieve.

"Your injuries have healed enough that you can shift out the rest," he said, carefully standing as if afraid moving too quickly would spook me... which it probably would. Just sitting he'd been intimidating and now, towering over me, he was terrifying.

"There's a bathroom across the hall. Why don't you get cleaned up and I'll find you some clothes." My stomach growled, making his lips quirk. "And some food," he added as he opened the door revealing a glimpse of another white wall and the edge of a door-frame. "I'm Cyrus."

"Audrey," I murmured and he left before I could thank him.

I didn't know why he was helping me or if I could actually trust him. Just because he wasn't connected to Sterling didn't mean I was safe with him. Of course, if he'd wanted to hurt me, he'd had plenty of opportunity while I was unconscious.

I sat up and pushed back the covers, my body throbbing in protest, the pain strong enough to cut through the cold emptiness. Someone had changed me out of my transformation dress, wrapped bandages around most of my torso, and put me in an oversized, loose shirt. Probably Cyrus.

I wasn't sure how I felt about that. I'd never been naked in public before. Hell, I'd never been naked in private with another person. But he was a shifter and not from my pack, so he probably didn't have the human hang-ups I did about nudity. Royce had already ripped open the front of my dress so I'd probably been flashing it all when he'd found me.

My throat tightened at the thought of my dress. That dress had held all my hopes for the last five years. It was gone and so was the life I knew.

I couldn't go back, even if for some ridiculous reason I wanted to. I could only go forward and to do that I needed to figure out where I was and how to get farther away from Sterling. I could only pray that as a wolfless shifter I'd be able to go unnoticed or that he wouldn't bother searching for me. Although I had a horrible feeling that if he knew I was still alive, nothing would stop him from coming after me.

And again, there was nothing I could do about that right now.

I climbed out of bed and headed to the bathroom — which was right across the hall like Cyrus said. The room was luxurious with white marble floors, counters, and tiles, and shiny chrome fixtures. An enormous mirror sat over the vanity, and I cringed at my reflection.

My not-blond-but-not-brown hair hung half loose in a tangled mess while the rest was still captured at an odd angle in the hair elastic I'd used for my ponytail. I also had two black eyes and was covered in bruises and scratches, although they weren't nearly as fresh as they should have been, which meant I had to have been unconscious for more than a day.

A large tub sat at the back in a bay window that looked out onto a small garden, and while I really wanted to just soak and relax, Cyrus had promised food and I was hungry.

I started the water in the stand-up shower, which was more than big enough for a man Cyrus's size, and grabbed the hem of the shirt. It was enormous on me, hanging past my butt, and would have been loose on Cyrus, but that only meant it would be quick to take off.

Was that a clue about the type of man Cyrus was? He anticipated he'd need to shift at a moment's notice and wore clothes that were easy to take off since our shifting magic destroyed whatever we wore?

I pulled the shirt up over my head and was instantly enveloped in that rich, smoky scent again. God, it smelled so good. Like home... even though I hadn't thought I associated home with wood smoke.

The icy hollowness inside me shuddered and the warm comfort of the scent turned into longing and need. I ached to be surrounded by that scent forever, to be fully embraced by it, have it fuel my need into a burning desire, and set me fully ablaze. I didn't want to discard the shirt on the floor, step into the shower, and wash the scent from my skin. My soul ached for it to accept me, welcome me home, caress me, touch me, love me.

A part of me knew I felt the way I did because of the incomplete mating bond, but another, smaller part, a part I'd been ignoring and denying because I'd had to survive, knew deep down the incomplete bond only shone a light on what I'd desperately craved from the moment I found my father in a pool of his own blood in the bathtub.

Tears burned my eyes and I tossed the shirt to the farthest corner of the bathroom.

Fuck you, Royce, for making me feel this way. Fuck you for reminding me that I was broken and no one wanted me.

Those horrible feelings had been dragged into the stark light of reality and even when the icy emptiness of the incomplete mating bond faded, I'd never be able to forget about how I longed for something I couldn't have.

So clearly pointing out what I ached for was the cruelest thing he'd ever done to me.

Fuck you and Sterling. Fuck all of them.

My throat tightened.

And fuck me for being stupid enough to believe them.

A tear rolled down my cheek and I furiously brushed it away. I didn't want to cry. I didn't want to be emotionally pathetic as well.

But the tears kept leaking from my eyes, my soul and body weeping despite my mind's determination to be strong.

Damn it. I'd had a plan. I'd finally worked up the nerve to leave whether my wolf woke or not. I'd been cautious to leave the pack because, weak as I was, I thought I'd be in more danger out there than staying where I was, but I'd never just given up.

I couldn't have been more wrong about being safe with Sterling and Royce the psychopaths.

Cautious had nearly gotten me killed.

Shame burned my cheeks and anger flickered, a miniscule flame, in the icy hollowness in my chest.

God, I wanted to rip off Royce's and Sterling's cocks and feed them to that monster. But they were stronger than me in every way. Ridiculously so.

The most I'd be able to accomplish would be yelling at them and then they'd probably kill me.

Resigned with the burning knowledge that life really wasn't fair, I unwrapped the bandage around my chest.

Wads of bloody gauze plopped on the floor, a testament to how injured I'd been. Royce's claw marks were ugly red gashes down the front of my chest, and without the ability to shift, they'd scar. I'd have a permanent reminder of his betrayal not just hidden in my soul but sliced into my skin for any future lover to see. Hell, even a low-cut neckline would show them off to everyone.

My throat tightened again with emotions I really didn't want, and I stepped into the shower and leaned my forehead against the tiles, just letting the warm water stream down my back. If I was smart, I'd hurry up and clean myself. The more I stood still, the more the icy hollowness would affect me, and a part of me was afraid it would be too much and I'd give up, just like my father had.

He and my mother hadn't been fated mates and they hadn't created a magical mating bond, but I'd gotten the impression from him and everyone around me that they'd loved each other deeply. Her love and support had been what had held him together and kept the nightmares at bay when he'd returned to the pack after the war.

Logically I knew he'd held on for as long as he could after her death before the nightmares had become too much and he'd killed himself. But there was still a little girl inside me who felt abandoned, felt she hadn't been enough for him, and was afraid she had the same emotional weakness he'd had.

My shifter essence was weak. Why not the rest of me?

I shoved those thoughts as deep down inside me as

possible. I hadn't lost my love and hadn't survived years of brutal war. I'd had the shit scared out of me for a few hours and been tricked by an asshole. Killing myself would just be letting him win, and I was *not* going to let him win. I'd survive just to spite him and Sterling and everyone.

AUDREY

Determined to ignore the icy hollowness until it went away — because it was *going* to go away — I grabbed the bar of soap on the small ledge at the back of the shower and worked it into a lather. I washed the grime from my hair and picked out the tangles as best I could without conditioner, then turned my attention to my body.

Just reaching up to my head pulled at the gashes in my torso. The wounds on my front had healed enough that they wouldn't open up if I scrubbed too hard — and I suspected the wounds on my back were the same — but that didn't mean they weren't tender.

I ran my soapy hands over my chest, carefully washing away the dried blood without hurting myself. If I closed my eyes, I could almost pretend I was having a shower like normal.

Except the moment I did, I became hyperaware of the hollowness inside me. It was icy and aching and thrumming with longing that grew with every slide of my hands.

The edge of my palm brushed my nipple and the longing swelled, oozing heat into the cold, making me ache for a touch that was never coming.

It was just another thing that was cruel about tricking me into starting the mating vows and then leaving me hanging. A mating bond heightened sexual desire and I had no one to be sexual with... well there was Cyrus.

Even if he was intimidating, he was handsome. Maybe he'd be interested in a little something. I knew in my heart it wouldn't be the same as having sex with my mate, but since I didn't have a mate—

Oh, my God! What was I thinking?

Even if he was interested, I didn't know him. Did I really want to have sex with a stranger just to relieve the pressure? Worse yet, did I want to have sex *for the first time* with a stranger just to relieve the pressure? How did I even go about asking for that?

You're cute and I'm a horny virgin, you wanna...?

Jeez. The situation wasn't that bad. I could barely feel anything. Really... even if I was getting hornier by the second.

No. I was *not* going to ask Cyrus to have sex with me.

If things got too bad, I'd just take care of myself by myself. I'd done that before. It would be enough to get me through the worst of it while the incomplete bond faded away.

And now I was also determined to ignore the aching longing. A few more things to ignore and I'd have to change my middle name to Denial.

I scrubbed down as quickly as possible, not caring that I aggravated my injuries — pain was better than the aching longing — and hurried out of the shower. I'd just finished drying myself off and was trying to figure out what to do about clothing since the only thing I had to wear was the towel or the shirt that I didn't — and did — want to put back on when someone knocked on the door.

"Clothing," Cyrus said, and he opened the door a crack and set a pile of silky blue fabric on the floor along with a pair of strappy tan sandals.

I picked up the fabric and it unfurled into a backless dress that was secured at the nape of the neck and the small of the back with ties. It hung to my ankles and covered everything it was supposed to cover, but I still felt naked wearing it. The soft fabric clung to every curve and without a bra, I couldn't hide my peaked nipples. I could only hope Cyrus thought I was cold and not turned on like I really was.

Why in God's name would he give me a dress like that? Had I been wrong about his intentions?

And damn if it didn't make it even harder to pretend the only thing I was feeling from the mating bond was cold emptiness.

I stepped out of the bathroom and Cyrus's eyes narrowed, making me cross my arms over my chest, even more uncomfortable in the flimsy dress than before.

"You won't get pity walking around like that," he said, his voice still gruff and now edged with a hint of frustration. "You might as well shift out the rest of your injuries."

"I'm not looking for pity." But I also didn't want to tell him that I couldn't shift. He might have saved my life but that didn't mean I could trust him, especially if he learned how weak I really was. "I appreciate you saving me."

"Want to tell me what you were doing in Darkweald to begin with?" he asked, striding down the hall, forcing me to scramble to catch up.

"Darkweald?" I didn't recognize the name. How far had the stream washed me away? I thought I was familiar with the names of everything on and around pack lands.

Of course, I didn't remember a stream anywhere near the sacred grove... and I wasn't sure what to think about that.

The hall opened into a grand front entrance with an enormous glittering chandelier, massive front doors, and a thick, red rug. We stood on the second level at the edge of an equally grand staircase that started split in two on the ground level, curving up and around a wide entrance, met again halfway up creating a broad landing, and split again to the hall where Cyrus and I stood and to another hall across from us, suggesting the building had two wings.

Every surface was clean and well kept, just like the bathroom and the room I'd woken in. This wasn't some abandoned mansion Cyrus had found and was squatting in while he passed by, and it didn't seem like a bed and breakfast or short-term rental, either. It was too… grand for something like that.

Except that didn't make any sense.

There wasn't a mansion like this anywhere near pack lands. Even if I'd never gone beyond the area owned by the pack, I would have heard from the others about a house like this, occupied or otherwise.

Of course, if I'd been unconscious for a few days, we could have easily driven across the state. Which meant I could be one step closer to getting as far away from Sterling, Royce, and that monster as possible.

"Yes, Darkweald," Cyrus pressed, leading me down the stairs.

The entrance that was framed by the split stairs opened into a large empty room lit by indirect sunlight coming through dozens of windows. They were smaller than expected, looking like they belonged to a much older building. But I didn't get a chance to get a good look before Cyrus headed away from the grand entrance down a wide hall and took me to a kitchen big enough for a medium-sized restaurant.

There were dozens more of the smallish windows

along the far wall, but these faced a different direction and full sunlight streamed through. A door at the back stood open, letting in more sunlight along with a warm, fresh breeze fragrant with the scent of flowers and herbs, and beyond lay a garden, a tall stone wall, and a towering mountain.

I was still in the mountains so he hadn't taken me two days east. I might not be as far away from Sterling as I'd hoped, which meant I needed to figure out how to get moving.

With literally nothing, possibly not even the scraps of dress I'd been wearing for the transformation ceremony, I was going to have to walk across the country and rely on the kindness of strangers to survive. That, or find work to earn enough for a bus ticket to get me to Union City.

"Well?" A hint of his power rolled into me with that word.

I opened my mouth to answer him but managed to snap it shut before the truth poured out. Even if I lied about my age and said I was performing my pack's transformation ceremony, he'd still know exactly who my pack was, and I couldn't risk him trying to take me back.

Could I even mention being betrayed and almost sacrificed to a monster?

My cheeks burned with shame.

For all I knew, this guy might think he'd get a reward for returning me.

"You're not strong enough to resist me," he said,

opening a tall cupboard and revealing a strange looking fridge inside.

Swell. Of course, he'd just force me to talk. That was what powerful supers did to weaker ones, which only reminded me that I hadn't stood a chance in my pack, and I wouldn't in the real world, either.

AUDREY

My throat tightened and the icy emptiness inside me swelled. "I'm not strong enough for anything," I replied, moving toward the light pouring through the open back door, hoping that the warm air would ease the frozen ache.

"So?" Cyrus asked, but he didn't add more power to his word, giving me the chance to respond of my own free will, surprising me.

"I trusted someone I shouldn't have." I stepped into the sunlight and turned my face to the sky to stare up at two moons.

My thoughts stuttered. Two.

I squeezed my eyes shut, but when I opened them again, the moons were still there.

What the hell?

"Don't make me force you," Cyrus said

A hint of power returned to his words, and I was

about to open my mouth again when a man, more hand-some than Cyrus and almost as tall and muscular rounded a large bush in the garden.

His warm brown eyes widened with surprise when he saw me, and he flashed a smile that would have stopped my heart if it hadn't already been stopped with shock over the two moons.

"You're awake." His gaze swept over my face and his smile faltered, making me cringe. From the essence radiating off him he was as powerful — or awfully darn close to being as powerful — as Cyrus. And while he didn't look as intimidating, that didn't mean he wasn't going to use his power to force me to talk.

"Why didn't you shift?" he asked, his tone filled with concern and not reproach like Cyrus. "Your injuries have healed enough. It's safe."

"I'm not so sure about that." I pointed at the moons. "I'm seeing double."

Except the moons were clearly two distinct objects, one white and normal looking, the other slightly pink and smaller. Not to mention nothing else was doubled.

"I'm still unconscious. That's what this is— Or dead." No, if I was dead, I wouldn't have the icy emptiness threatening to consume me or the constant, throbbing whisper of need beneath that cold.

"You look conscious to me," the new guy said. He glanced up, looking for what I was looking at, but from his lack of reaction, he clearly didn't see anything wrong.

"If you don't see it then this has to be a dream."

"See what?" Cyrus growled.

I pointed up. "Two moons."

The new guy glanced behind me, his now weak smile melting into concern. "What about the moons?"

What about the moons! "There are *two* of them."

"And?" Cyrus huffed.

"Proving this is a dream and I'm unconscious somewhere bleeding to death."

"I don't understand how the Sisters prove you're dreaming," the new guy said.

"They even have a name." Of course they did. Because dreams were like that.

Except I had no idea where I'd come up with the two-moon thing. I didn't read or watch a whole lot of science fiction or fantasy so I doubted my subconscious would gravitate towards something like that, and nothing else about this felt like a dream...

Was I in another realm?

There were a number of portals all over the planet. Some led to a specific realm like the one in Rome which only went to the Realm of Celestial Light, but there were others that could go to any number of realms if you had enough power and the right spell or the right kind of super with you.

I turned to Cyrus. "Where did you take me?"

There wasn't a portal anywhere near pack lands, but there was at least one within a two-day drive.

And if I was in another realm, did that mean I was safe? It was farther than I thought I could ever get from

Sterling, but I didn't know much about the other realms and had no idea how dangerous this one might be.

"You're in Stonehaven," Cyrus said, filling a glass with water at the sink.

"No, what realm?"

The new guy frowned. "Are you saying you're from another realm?" He pulled out a chair at a nearby table and gestured for me to sit.

I frowned back at him. If he didn't know I was from the mortal realm then— "You didn't bring me here?"

"We found you in Darkweald forest." Cyrus set a plate with a sandwich along with the glass of water in front of me then sat in the chair opposite me. His dark green eyes locked on me and power rolled off him, making my insides tremble, but he didn't push — not yet at least — and force me to talk.

"You were badly hurt," the new guy murmured, taking the seat beside me.

Then realization hit me. If I was in a different realm, I must have gone through the portal Sterling had made to summon that monster. That monster was from this realm.

My pulse leaped, suddenly racing. Was I safe here from that thing?

Oh, my God! Were there more of them?

If there were more of them maybe these guys knew how to defend against them. They were certainly strong shifters. Stronger than Sterling and Royce. Maybe a monster like that was nothing to them.

The new guy brushed his fingers across the back of my hand, jerking my attention— hell, my whole essence to him. He was so close I could see the green flecks in his warm brown eyes.

"You're safe," he said, his voice soft and soothing, easing some of the panic.

But that only made me aware of his fingers on my skin, the heat radiating from his body, easily seeping through my thin dress, and the aching longing thrumming in my soul.

I struggled to focus beyond my growing need. "You know how to kill those monsters?"

A hint of concern flickered in the new guy's eyes.

"What monsters?" Cyrus asked.

"It looked like a greater demon in his natural form but all red like a movie monster." And it had started eating Merrick while he was still alive.

I shuddered and my gaze dipped to the sandwich Cyrus had made me as my stomach churned.

"None of what you just said made any sense," Cyrus said.

"I've read about greater demons," the new guy replied. "Whil has a book that mentions them. But I don't know what this movie monster is."

"It's—" How did I explain? Did they even have photography here or would it be easier to compare it to a painting or a play?

Except that wasn't the point. Confirming that these

men knew about the monster and were capable of dealing with it was.

"It was big and red with horns and claws and ate people," I said.

The muscles in Cyrus's jaw flexed but he didn't react as if he knew what I was talking about, and the new guy's eyes grew bigger.

"Do you think—?" the new guy started, but Cyrus shot him a hard look, stopping him mid sentence.

"We need to talk to Whil," Cyrus said.

AUDREY

CYRUS STOOD AND HEADED TO THE BACK DOOR, STILL OPEN and still letting the sunlight pour into the kitchen.

"So you don't know how to kill it?" I asked. Which meant there weren't dozens of those monstrous things wandering around this realm.

The new guy stood and motioned for me to follow Cyrus. Practicality made me grab my sandwich even though I was no longer hungry. I still had no idea what I was doing or where I was going, but I couldn't afford to do anything on an empty stomach, especially if I hadn't eaten in a couple of days.

Outside, I turned my face to the sun, hoping it would warm more than just my skin, but the warmth couldn't penetrate the frozen emptiness inside me, and I feared nothing ever would.

The other guy — whose name I still had to learn — drew up close behind me, too close for my comfort even though I was a shifter and as a species we had a smaller personal space than most. But I couldn't tell if he was close because his personal space with strangers was practically non-existent or for some other reason.

From the outside, the mansion looked more like a Medieval castle, made from large stone blocks. It stood three stories — four or five stories at the six turrets — and was surrounded by gardens and a high wall.

Beyond the wall, I could see a few more buildings tucked against the rise of the mountain and suspected there were more on the other side of the mansion. These buildings were plainer, more practical than the castle, but still made from large stone blocks, and past them stood an even taller wall.

Then we rounded a corner and stepped into a shaded grove. It wasn't very big, not like my pack's— my *old* pack's sacred grove in the middle of the forest, but with the trees clustered in a circle and pruned so their branches in the center framed the sky, it was clearly a grove.

Cyrus led us around the grove and down a slope to a strange building that was half English cottage and half greenhouse tucked against the large protective wall. Bushes and trees and vines crowded around the building and everything was in bloom regardless of their season, spring irises and tulips blooming beside fragrant roses and black-eyed Susans.

Something flickered at the edge of my vision... or was that the edge of my senses. It tugged at me, pulling my attention from the impossible cottage to the shadows in the grove above.

The icy emptiness shuddered and the aching need swelled.

I was suddenly hyperaware of the new guy, his muscular body close behind me. It was as if I could feel his body heat, which was impossible since he wasn't *that* close. But he was even more handsome than Cyrus and with that smile of his and his kinder attitude, he'd be an even better choice to alleviate the need caused by my incomplete mating bond.

"Whil," Cyrus called out, stopping at the cottage's open door and surprising me. He struck me as the kind of man who'd just barge in and make demands. He was more than powerful enough to be the alpha of a pack, and in my experience wolves that powerful didn't ask, they took.

"In the library," a feminine voice called back.

"Our guest is awake," he said, not going into the house as expected, but heading around to the greenhouse part and stepping through an open door from one garden bursting with life to another one.

Interspersed among the vines and branches and leaves and blooms were shelves crammed with books and jars and scrolls. The floor — wide flagstones when there was floor and not moss or grass or other groundcover — was set in wide steps, except they didn't go in one direction. There were a few going up on the right to a tall bookcase and a few going down to a bench while another two steps were raised in the center of a small pool.

The room was larger than I expected, and we wandered to the back where there were more bookcases, fewer windows — although the ceiling was still glass — and a mismatched seating arrangement that consisted of a short, old-fashioned couch with only one arm, a more modern looking chair with thick cushions, two more simpler chairs, and a stool.

On the floor, surrounded by uneven piles of books, sat the most beautiful woman I'd ever seen. She was so stunning she seemed to glow, caught in a perpetual stream of sunlight that haloed her entire body, made her long golden hair shimmer, and accentuated the delicate tips of her pointed ears.

My breath caught. She wasn't just a woman, she was a fae woman. And from how pointed her ears were, she had to be full fae.

"Am I in Faerie?" I asked, my voice breathy with awe.

The fae had sent a few sorcerers to help with the war, but they'd kept to themselves and very few people had actually seen one. The only evidence that they had even helped were the few faekin — men and women who were half-fae — wandering around the mortal realm. There were only a few pictures of a few faekin on the internet, never any fae, and only one faekin sat in the Joined Parliament.

The woman raised a sculpted eyebrow and glanced at Cyrus as he sat on the couch. The movement exuded power and danger, and I doubted he was purposely trying to intimidate me. This was his natural state. A predator.

"She thinks she's from a different realm," Cyrus replied.

I shot him a dark look. "I don't think. I know. My realm doesn't have two moons."

Cyrus matched my dark look and let a hint of power roll over me. "You could be lying."

"Why would I be lying?"

"Come here." The woman — what had Cyrus called her? Whil? — pushed the books in front of her aside to make room for me on the floor. "You're not in Faerie, but I am fae. I'm Whiltierna. Everyone calls me Whil."

"Audrey," I said, stepping over a small pile of books to get to her.

Whil held out her hand, palm up. "The boys found you in Darkweald."

"That's what Cyrus keeps saying," I replied, sitting in front of her and placing my hand in hers.

Golden light radiated from her skin and a warm caress of power curled over my hand and up my arm.

"A malicious god sleeps in Darkweald. You could have gone there with evil intentions," she said.

I huffed, and the power seeped over my shoulder and into my chest. It oozed around my heart, soft and sensual, but couldn't get past the ice to fill the emptiness inside me.

Nothing would fill it. I was going to be broken and empty forever.

I tried to push that thought aside.

It will fade. It has to fade.

"Oh child," the woman breathed. "That's a nasty curse."

Both of the men leaned forward.

"Did she get it from Tzanagoth?" Cyrus asked.

"No, this is old. Handed down from generation to generation." The woman raised a gaze filled with sadness and captured me with eyes the color of new leaves.

My cheeks heated with embarrassment. One quick look and she knew I couldn't shift.

"Did you go to Darkweald to use Tzanagoth's power to break your curse?" Cyrus pressed.

"No," I said.

His power rolled over me, stronger than before.

"I'm from the mortal realm," I insisted, my body bending forward of its own volition to submit to him. "I don't know what Darkweald is or anything about this Tzanagoth."

Whil shot Cyrus a look and his power vanished. "How do you know about the realms?" she asked.

"Supers—"

She frowned at me.

"Supernatural beings," I corrected. Guess she wasn't familiar with the short form. "We came out of hiding about twenty-five years ago when the archangel Michael decided to cleanse the earth of the *human infestation*. The entire planet learned in one horrible attack that angels and the Realm of Celestial Light were real and so was almost everything else."

The new guy pulled the stool closer to me and sat. "Everything?"

"They didn't go into a whole lot of detail in school, but yeah. There are hundreds of realms, maybe thousands—"

"And you can learn about them later, Bishop," Cyrus said, cutting me off. "We need to know what happened, and we need—" Cyrus snapped his mouth shut, cutting himself off.

Clearly, I wasn't supposed to know whatever that second bit was.

The other guy — Bishop — sighed. "So, what did happen?"

I was stupid enough to think Royce was my fated mate and had trusted him too easily. And I still had no idea what Cyrus's intentions were.

"Two guys from my pack summoned a monster and tried to sacrifice me to it," I said, not wanting to get into all the embarrassing details but knowing I needed to say enough so they'd think I'd told them everything. "The alpha interrupted them and it tossed me aside to eat him. I wasn't thinking clearly. I was bleeding and hit my head so I'm not quite sure what happened, but I think I ran through the portal the thing came out of to get to the mortal realm."

There. Straight to the point. Everything they need to know without all the embarrassing details.

My gaze dipped to the sandwich still in my free hand and Merrick's screams shuddered through me, making my stomach heave.

"It ate him," I murmured, the words slipping out.

"Who?" Whil asked.

"The alpha. It started ripping him apart and eating him while he was still alive."

More of Whil's power seeped into me, pressing against the icy barrier but unable to break through. "How did they open the portal to summon it?" she asked.

"I don't know. They poured a potion on the ground and there was black mist and lightning."

"Just a potion?" Whil's grip on my hand tightened. "There had to be something else."

Yeah, an incomplete mating bond.

Whil's gaze flickered up to Cyrus and his power surged over me.

"There's more," he growled. "Tell her."

I bent over, my forehead pressed against the flag-stones in forced submission. "The alpha mentioned something from his safe," I gasped.

"What was it?" Whil asked.

"I don't know."

"You're hiding something," she insisted. "I've cast an intention spell and I know there's something you're not telling us."

AUDREY

THE PRESSURE FROM CYRUS'S POWER GREW, CRUSHING inside my frozen chest. "I won't let you endanger my pack," he said, his voice low. "If someone from your world woke and summoned Tzanagoth, someone here could figure it out, too. What are you hiding?"

"It's not important." *Please.* I didn't want to say it. I didn't want to confess I was so weak and desperate that I'd believed someone powerful like Royce was destined for me.

But Cyrus's power kept growing and it didn't matter how hard I clenched my jaw, the words still poured out. "An incomplete mating bond. They needed an incomplete mating bond."

The pressure vanished and the icy emptiness roared back in. "The only way for that to happen—" Cyrus said not needing to finish his sentence.

He was a shifter. If he knew about mating bonds, then

he knew I was stupid enough to initiate one and was then rejected.

"Yeah." My throat tightened with emotions I really didn't want, and I collapsed forward, sobbing, the shame and frustration and aching cold too much to hold back.

It will pass. It will pass. Please, God, make it pass.

It's not going to pass, a voice filled with burning anger snarled in my head.

It will. It has to. If it didn't, I had no idea how I was going to hold out. I already teetered dangerously close to the edge of complete surrender. I didn't know how much longer I could hold out before the incomplete mating bond made me think the only way out was death.

I hadn't thought the grief would be so strong. It was just incomplete, a connection between my soul and Royce's hadn't been made so I shouldn't have felt as if a piece of myself had been ripped out.

It won't. It isn't incomplete, the voice growled.

What? How?

But the second he said it, I knew it was true. I could feel the bond around my heart, partially woven into my soul, and I could sense it was linked—

Oh, God.

It was linked to whoever was speaking in my head. I didn't even know who he was. He didn't sound like Cyrus or Bishop. But I recognized his scent, the dark rich aroma of wood smoke, and every cell in my being knew he was mine. Forever. My mate.

I felt cold and empty not because the bond was

incomplete, but because he'd frozen our connection. He didn't want me and was fighting the bond with everything he had.

My gaze jerked across the greenhouse to a large, black wolf stalking across the uneven floor toward me.

"Why?" I gasped. It didn't make sense. If he didn't want the bond, why accept it? *Why say the other half of the vow and finish it?*

I didn't. He curled his lips back, baring his long canines, and growled at me. *I refuted you and you forced it on me anyway.*

"I what?" How could I have done that? Even if I'd been aware of what I was doing, I wouldn't have been able to force the bond on him. He had to say the vow and accept it.

You forced it on me. He captured my gaze with his strange black eyes, and I knew, through the bond he didn't want, that he meant every word he said. *I don't want it and I don't want you.*

His words shot ice into my heart with an agony more painful than anything I'd experienced before.

I was nothing, weak, unwanted. Not even my mate wanted me. He didn't want me with every fiber of his being.

His hate and anger tore into my soul deeper than his claws could have. It would have been less painful if he'd attacked me.

"Not true," I gasped. "It's not true."

It is, my mate snarled.

No. It couldn't be. *I am worthy. I deserve to be loved. I'm stronger than this.*

But the icy hollowness crushed inside me. I couldn't catch my breath. I kept gasping, kept trying to draw in air, but it wasn't enough. Nothing was going to be enough.

I scrambled to my feet. I needed space, air. *God, please. Why can't I breathe?*

The pressure from Cyrus's power crashed over me. He said something, but I couldn't understand his words, could barely hear anything beyond the rushing in my head and the anguish in my heart.

My mate didn't want me.

No one wanted me.

I didn't want to feel that way. I shouldn't. I was strong enough to survive living with Sterling and strong enough to survive almost being sacrificed to a monster. I could survive this. I just needed to get away from them, away from *him*, from everything, and breathe.

I staggered, fell to one knee, pushed back up, and kept going toward the door.

I had to escape this madness, even though I knew there was no escape. No, that wasn't true. There were two ways to escape. His death or mine, and given his strength and the strength of the others around me, it was going to be mine.

I should just give up, stop fighting, and face the inevitable. I might have escaped that monster, but I couldn't escape this. My only way out was death. I couldn't even run away. Even if I could somehow evade my mate, the emptiness and anguish would always be with me.

And yet my body kept trying to escape, trying to find enough space within me to breathe, because a small, desperate voice inside me was certain that if I could just breathe, I'd be able to fight the overwhelming emotions. *Please, I need to breathe.*

"Stop," Cyrus roared, his voice cutting through the rushing in my head.

His power surged and dropped me to both knees, but my body kept fighting, crawling even as the pressure pushed me down. I needed to escape.

God, why had I been so stupid?

BISHOP

THE WOMAN, AUDREY, HEAVED AGAINST CYRUS'S CONTROL even as I tried to get him to stop. Tears streamed down her cheeks, her expression filled with the terror and anguish of a panic attack, making my heart break for her. Then a glittering stream of golden magic caressed the back of her head and she passed out, put to sleep by Whil's spell.

"What's wrong with you?" I demanded, glaring at Cyrus and giving him one last mental shove with my power, drawing an *oomph* but doing little else. "You didn't have to force her to tell us about the incomplete bond and you certainly didn't have to force her to stay. I could have caught up to her outside, and I could have gotten her to tell us everything without terrorizing her."

"And I needed to know she wasn't a threat." Cyrus snarled back.

"Well, she's not." And it had been obvious the

moment I'd looked at her, broken and bleeding, in the river. She hadn't deserved what had happened to her. No one had.

"And you," I said, shooting my glare at Knox before picking her up and cradling her in my arms. "She just confessed she had an incomplete mating bond as part of what happened to her, which means those men who tried to kill her either murdered her mate before they could finish saying their vows or one of them made her fall in love with him then betrayed her." And I wasn't sure which made me angrier. Both were horrible.

I jerked my chin at Cyrus, telling him to get off the couch, so I could set Audrey on it.

I was trying to break the bond, Knox growled, a hint of regret whispering through our bond before he clamped down on it. *Get her to refute it with me.*

"Without telling her what you were doing?" I asked as Cyrus got out of my way. "She's just had her heart broken and you told her you didn't want her."

I don't.

"But you didn't prepare her. All you did was flood her with rejection without warning while the bond is telling her you're supposed to love her." I laid her on the couch but didn't want to let her go and couldn't pull my attention away from her to keep glaring at my brothers... not that a hard look would change their minds. I was the flighty brother, the one who jumped from idea to idea, the flirt, the one who'd rather make a joke than an enemy and they both saw that as a weakness.

That only proves how weak she is. She didn't even try to fight back, Knox snarled.

"We don't know what her story is," I insisted, more pieces of my heart breaking. "Someone tried to kill her and she just lost her mate." And got an asshole in his place.

On top of that, her essence was weak. Depending on if her weakness was something she'd been born with or had for a long time — and with Whil's comment about a curse that might be true — fighting back might have never been an option for her, so it might not be a first instinct for her.

"After that little demonstration of *affection*," I said to Knox, "I have no doubt she'll be more than willing to try to break the mating bond with you."

Cyrus turned to Whil. "Did anything she say explain how she bonded with him without either of them saying anything?"

"No, and this bond can't be broken with just intention," Whil said, sitting on the edge of the couch and laying a hand on Audrey's forehead. "As much as I hoped it wasn't, now that I've gotten a better look at it, I know it's a real mating bond, not something else masquerading as one as I'd hoped. You might not have sealed it yet, but it already runs deep between you."

I don't care how strong it is. Find a way to break it. Knox's lips curled back and he growled at Audrey. *She's not my mate. She never was and never will be. I won't accept her. Ever.*

He stormed from the cottage, a flicker of furious emotions rushing through me before he clamped down on our bond as well.

"So that's it, then?" I asked. She was going to be stuck with my brother for the rest of her life when she'd thought she was going to spend it with the man she loved.

"Not necessarily," Whil replied. "It didn't form in the natural way so there's still a chance there was something about what happened to her that might be a key to breaking it. But the odds aren't good."

"I don't want to lose him because of some woman," Cyrus said. "And I don't want him stuck with someone we can't trust."

"She told the truth about what happened to her," Whil said, brushing a lock of hair away from Audrey's eyes. "And my intention spell confirmed that she told us everything she knew about how that monster, which I assume was Tzanagoth, was summoned." She frowned. "Although I'm not entirely sure he was actually summoned."

"Still," Cyrus said, a small wave of power rolling off him like it did when he was worried and not paying attention to controlling himself. "She didn't shift out her injuries. She's clearly trying to manipulate us."

Whil sighed and moved her hand from Audrey's head to over her heart. "She didn't shift out her injuries because she can't. That's the curse."

Cyrus stared at Whil as if he couldn't believe what

she'd just said then groaned and rubbed his face, suddenly looking exhausted and a little guilty. "Of course she can't. This just keeps getting better and better. Knox would rather stay in wolf form and now has a mate who doesn't even have a wolf form. They don't even have that in common."

"Can you break the curse?" I sat on the floor beside the couch near Audrey's head. How much suffering could one woman take? The person she loved was gone, her home was gone, and she couldn't shift. I couldn't imagine not having a connection with the wolf half of my soul and not being able to shift.

"There's a way to unlock it, but the release mechanism is damaged... maybe blocked? I'm not sure." Whil closed her eyes and raised her chin, a sign that she was using her magical senses to get a better look at the curse. "It's woven into every cell in her body. Even if I were in Faerie, I wouldn't have enough power to break it. A master sorcerer might, but I'm not a master sorcerer."

"And not what we should be worrying about," Cyrus said, squaring his shoulders and putting on his "alpha of the pack" expression, the same one Mom used to wear when she needed to ignore her emotions for the good of the pack. "We need to break the mating bond without killing either of them and figure out if we're in danger from Tzanagoth. I'm not willing to bet the safety of the pack thinking that the malicious god is now in Audrey's realm."

"I wouldn't bet that, either," Whil said. "The portals to

the other realms were locked by powerful magic. Two shifters wouldn't have enough power to break that lock, not even harnessing the magic within a mating bond, which is what sounds like happened."

"So then what?" Cyrus asked. "The monster was her imagination and she really didn't come from this other realm?"

"No. The spell could have opened a temporary crack or a rip between the realms. I'm not entirely sure how, but theoretically, with enough power and maybe the right spell, it's possible. But something as powerful as a god probably wouldn't have been able to pass through it. What attacked her alpha probably was a temporary manifestation of Tzanagoth." Whil picked her way through the piles of books to a shelf partially hidden by a flowering vine. "What I don't know is if summoning that temporary manifestation broke the sleeping spell on him or not."

"If he's still in our realm and now awake, wouldn't we have felt his presence?" I asked. Everything I'd read about the gods said they radiated a powerful essence when conscious and if he was awake, I doubted he'd have stayed within Anakar's ruins.

"We'll know more when the hunting party returns," Cyrus said. His gaze slid to Audrey and the muscles in his jaw flexed, and I could practically hear the wheels in his head turning as he tried to decide what to do with her and if it was worth the time to save our brother when our entire pack could be in danger.

And while I wanted to argue and tell him we couldn't lose Knox, I also understood that the pack came first. Even before family.

"I won't know what to look for regarding Tzanagoth until we hear from the hunting party," Whil said before Cyrus could make the difficult decision to let Knox and Audrey suffer.

"You have until then," he replied then turned his attention to me. "Take care of her. Everything will be easier if she's not having a meltdown."

"You should have thought of that before you made her submit," I said.

"Don't start," he said, sending a wave of power washing over me. "You know I had to get the truth. We can't be divided on this. Not if we're going to keep Knox."

And as much as I hated it, he was right. It didn't matter what I thought of Audrey. She wasn't family and she wasn't at risk of going feral. Although from that panic attack it looked like there might be a chance she'd completely melt down and kill herself, a thought that had my wolf rising to the surface with the need to take over and protect her.

"If it comes down to it and we have to pick one or the other, we pick Knox." Cyrus's expression softened. "I don't like it, but if we lose Knox, I could lose you, too. Your twin bond is almost as strong as a mating bond even though it shouldn't be, and you were a mess the last time he went feral."

I hated that those were our choices, but I couldn't fight Cyrus on this. "Fine."

"Bring her to dinner." His gaze dropped to her and his expression softened even more. "We can introduce her to our betas and I can show her that I can be pleasant."

He left and I turned my attention back to Audrey. She looked at peace, but her cheeks were still damp from her tears and her face was still bruised from her ordeal. She'd already gone through so much. I didn't want to accept that our choices were her or Knox. There had to be a way to save both of them that didn't involve forcing them to accept their bond.

The only way we knew how to break a bond was if one half of the bond died but what about transferring it? It was often easier to redirect something than stopping it completely.

"Can a bond be transferred?" I asked.

Whil froze her hand hovering over a book about to take it off the shelf. "What are you thinking?"

"That it might be easier to redirect a spell than break it."

"And if it's possible, who would you suggest we redirect the mating bond to?" she asked. "It would need to happen soon. She and Knox aren't going to be able to resist the compulsion to seal the bond for long. There wouldn't be a lot of time for her and her new mate to get to know each other."

Yeah, and while I could ask someone to take the bond, that idea didn't sit well with me. It made my chest tighten with a confusing mix of emotions. She was Knox's mate and I could feel their connection. The desire from their bond seeped through our twin bond and while it was only a fraction of what Knox was fighting, it added to my wolf's desire to protect her, hold her, love her—

"I already have a connection with Knox. I can feel their bond," I said. "It would probably be easier to move the mating bond to me."

Whil looked at me and raised a sculpted eyebrow.

Yeah, I was coming up with another one of my ridiculous ideas.

Except it wasn't ridiculous. The situation wasn't Audrey's fault or Knox's and neither of them deserved to suffer. Knox didn't have the social skills — and didn't want them — to nurture an unexpected relationship, but I did, and from what I'd seen so far, Audrey seemed like a kind, genuine person who'd just gone through the worst day of her life. And my wolf wholeheartedly agreed with that assessment.

If she was willing, we could make it work, if, of course, it was possible to redirect Knox's half of the mating bond.

AUDREY

I woke to the bright scent of fresh-cut grass, flowers, and the rich aroma of damp dirt then realized I was still in Whil's strange greenhouse library. Above, through the leaves and branches and the glass ceiling, the sky was starting to darken, the precursor to night when it had been the middle of the day when I'd had that panic attack and passed out.

Bishop sat cross-legged on the floor beside me with his back against the couch and an enormous book in his lap. His head was tipped forward, but a few small braids at his temples kept his jaw-length hair out of his eyes. It was long enough that he could have tied it back with an elastic, but just like with the over-sized shirt I'd woken up in, the braids indicated he was prepared to shift at a moment's notice.

He raised his gaze to meet mine and for a second, I was drowning in his warm brown eyes. Mesmerizing green flecks caught the lamplight, pulling me in deeper and deeper, like just how I'd fallen into Royce's gaze when I'd heard the fated mating call.

"How do you feel?" he asked, his voice soft, sending a shiver of need rushing through me even though I doubted he intended his tone to be sensual.

Turned on, cold, ashamed and—

And a whole bunch of things I didn't want to think about.

"Awful. Cyrus didn't have to force me to bring up the mating bond," I said, focusing on the one thing that didn't have to do with me being weak or foolish or anything else. Anger I could do. Anger was safe.

He offered me a soft, sad smile. "Would you have said something otherwise?"

No. The sooner I forgot about that mistake the better, except— "I would have when I found out I was bonded with a complete stranger."

"I know this must be difficult for you, but if you can think of anything else that happened to you that might help."

"Help how? My mate bond bound me to a man I've never met before who despises me." The ice inside me swelled along with the memory of how much he didn't want me. "I don't think hashing out the details will help him understand."

He'd hate me even more once he knew the truth. It was bad enough he was stuck with a weak stranger for the rest of his life, it would be worse once he knew I was naive and stupid, too.

"Your bond with Knox didn't form the normal way so maybe there's a way to break it," Bishop said.

My chest tightened at my mate's name, but I couldn't tell if it was with desire or grief.

"His name is Knox? Do you know him? Does he—?" The pressure tightened. Not desire or grief. Fear. I was feeling fear. He was so angry with me, his fury ice in my veins, would he take out that rage on me? "Does he have a temper?"

Bishop's eyes darkened and his power shuddered around him, threatening to release before he regained control. "He'd never lay a finger on you," he said, jumping to the conclusion — and likely seeing the fear in my eyes — that I was worried my unwanted mate would be abusive. "My brother is angry and he usually goes off by himself when he's upset, but he can't get as far away as he wants with the mating bond newly formed and still unsealed."

The word *unsealed* turned some of the cold back into aching desire. The bond didn't care if he hated me or that it had been a mistake to bond with him. It needed to be sealed and that meant having sex... and if we didn't do something about it, eventually the bond would compel us to have sex whether we wanted to or not.

"He's your brother?" I asked, trying not to think about the inevitable sex or, if we somehow managed to resist the bond long enough, the insanity.

"And Cyrus," Bishop said.

And they'd taken me to an enormous building that had to be the alpha's residence. They'd also looked right at home in the kitchen, which meant one of them was this pack's alpha.

It had to be Cyrus. His power was enormous, and while I could sense the others were strong as well even though they were holding back, Bishop was too nice and Knox was too angry.

"So I've accidentally forced a mating bond on the alpha's brother." Just great. The weakest wolf in existence had forced herself into an alpha's family.

"It wasn't your fault. The bond was meant for someone else." Sadness filled Bishop's eyes, and for a second, I couldn't understand why. Then I realized he didn't know I'd been tricked. He thought my intended mate had been killed before he could finish our mating vows. "With luck we'll be able to find a way to break the bond and you can mourn properly."

I contemplated going with the lie. It would mean no one in this realm would know I'd been so foolish, but I was a horrible liar and I'd feel uncomfortable getting sympathy from everyone for a lover I hadn't lost.

"I wish it was like that," I said, my cheeks heating with shame. "I wish there'd been someone who'd wanted to mate with someone like me."

Bishop's sadness turned to knowing, but without any disgust like I'd feared. "I think being tricked into falling in love with someone might be worse."

"Yeah, the asshole is probably still alive and laughing at me," I said bitterly. And if I was stronger...

"How long did he play you along?" Whil asked, stepping out from behind a flowering shrub carrying a tray with a teapot and cups.

"Thankfully, not long. Somehow they found a witch who could make a spell or potion or something that imitated a fated mating call."

"A fated mating call?" Bishop asked as Whil set the tray on a nearby table.

Right. He didn't know what that was. That was something only my pack experienced. "It's a side-effect of the spell that—" My throat tightened. *Come on. Just say it. Whil has already sensed the truth.*

"A side-effect of the curse that prevents you from shifting," Whil finished for me, pouring tea into a cup and offering it to me.

I took the cup and stared into the pale green liquid. "A long time ago the alpha of the pack made a deal with a powerful witch to enspell us, or rather my ancestors. The wolf half of our soul is kept asleep until the summer solstice after our eighteenth birthday."

"Why would someone do that?" Bishop asked, horrified.

"Humans hadn't taken well to supers in our realm and it was a safety precaution. Unlike the other packs, we didn't have to worry about a child shifting where a human could see," I replied. "Because of that, we were able to have stronger connections with human communities, and my pack— *that* pack became one of the most powerful packs on the planet."

"And when your wolf finally wakes all the senses that had been repressed that you should have had a lifetime to acclimatize to, burst into existence," Whil said.

"Sometimes those senses lock onto a similar soul, a perfect mate," I said. "It's like— it *was* like fire and pressure and a vibration in my soul that shook my essence. I don't know if that's what it's supposed to feel like or not since it wasn't real." There were only a couple of fated mates in the pack, but I hadn't talked to them about the fated mating call, and all I had to go on were rumors about what it felt like.

"Sounds like an angelic mating brand," Whil said, leaving her cup of tea only half poured and heading to a bookshelf hidden behind a small tree with bright autumn leaves.

"I looked at Royce and I just *knew* he was my mate." I blew at the steam curling from my cup, my hands starting to tremble. "I didn't know him very well. I didn't have a lot of status in the pack before my eighteenth birthday, and when my wolf didn't wake, I lost even more status. Royce said—" I huffed a bitter laugh. Royce had said a lot of things that hadn't been true. "He said he was afraid the alpha would deny our mating. He was friends with the alpha's son and next in line to be the first beta."

"So you rushed to say your vows," Bishop said, some of the sadness returning to his expression with a huge helping of pity.

Swell. Although I should probably be happy it was pity and not disgust like how my pack looked at me. I'd tried every day to be better, stronger, enough, but that hadn't made my wolf wake or my pack treat me any differently.

"Then they cast the spell and summoned the monster and you know the rest." I tried to raise my cup to my lips to take a sip but my hands were shaking too much.

"Here." Bishop took my cup from me and set it back on the tray.

Why was I shaking? I couldn't figure out my reaction. Of course, all I could really feel was icy hollowness and aching yearning.

He captured my hands between his, his palms warm against my skin, and held my gaze with his warm brown eyes.

"How long have you been afraid?" he murmured.

"For as long as I can remember," I whispered. Even when my father had been alive, I'd been afraid. He'd yell in his sleep, lose his temper, break things. It was his bad memories and it hadn't been his fault, but my existence had always been precarious.

"Whether we break the bond or not, you're safe here." He brushed his thumb against my cheek and I realized I was crying. My body was finally reacting to the shock of what had happened, but I was too twisted up inside by the mating bond— or rather Knox *rejecting* the mating bond to feel it.

"I'm a shifter who can't shift. I don't have any value."

"Whoever told you that is dead wrong," Whil said from behind the tree. "We all have something to offer. I'm a sorcerer, but my ability to channel raw magical power from the Realm of Faerie is so small it's almost laughable to call me a sorcerer. But here in this realm, I'm a counselor and archivist and researcher. You just haven't figured out where you fit yet and it sounds like your previous pack didn't give you a chance to find out."

It sounded so easy when she said it like that and I desperately wanted it to be true, but I knew it wasn't so simple to be seen as something more than the girl who couldn't shift.

"Now let me do my work here. You have a dinner to go to," Whil said.

"Dinner?" I asked.

Bishop offered me a soft smile. "Cyrus wants to prove he isn't a complete asshole and has asked that you join us and our betas for dinner."

"I don't think that's a good idea." I really didn't want a repeat of being forced to submit, especially with a larger audience, and I didn't trust that Cyrus wouldn't do it. That and I still looked like I'd been beaten up, which would make people stare at me and ask questions I didn't want to answer. "I should stay and help Whil. Two heads are better than one, right?"

"Can you read Sennari, Common Fae, Latin, or Ofuin?" Whil asked.

"No." And I hadn't even heard of half those languages. Well so much for that. "I still think going to this dinner is a bad idea." I gestured to my face as if Bishop — who'd already figured out so much without me having to say anything — wouldn't have realized why I didn't want to meet other people.

"You can't avoid meeting our betas until you're fully healed. You'll be living in our house for a while, and they need to meet you right away so they don't think you're a threat." Bishop hooked his finger under my chin and brought my gaze back to his, making the aching need inside me swell. "And no, you're not living someplace else," he added before I could suggest the idea. "Even if you're only Knox's mate for a little while, you're still family right now."

"And if we can break the bond and I'm no longer Knox's mate?" I asked, holding his gaze.

"We'll help find a place for you, whether it's here at the Residence or in town."

The intensity in his eyes grew, fueling my need, and I broke eye contact, dropping my attention to my hands in my lap.

It sounded too good to be true. And maybe it was, but I didn't have any choice. I couldn't leave because the bond would compel me back to Knox so we could seal it whether we wanted to or not and it was already pretty insistent.

Even if the situation was half as good or a quarter as good as Bishop made it out to be that was still better than where I'd come from. I could live with that... if my bond with Knox didn't drive me insane first.

AUDREY

WE WENT STRAIGHT FROM WHIL'S COTTAGE TO A DINING room large enough to host fifty people, although the long table was only set for eight at the one end. The room wasn't the enormous one I'd seen from the front hall, that room had been the size of a ballroom— it probably *was* a ballroom. This was a "more intimate" dining room.

The thought made a hysterical laugh bubble in my throat and I tried to swallow it back. Merrick's house had been big, but it hadn't been a castle. It had one dining room for about ten people, and if he wanted to meet with more, he hosted them in the ballroom in the town's main hotel. Somehow, I'd gone from Cinderella trapped by a big fish in a tiny pond to Cinderella at the end of the story in a castle. The only thing I didn't have was a prince.

I glanced at Bishop as he led me to a chair two seats down from the head of the table and pulled it out for me.

Maybe I did have a prince. Although being nice to me didn't mean he was interested and I was also mated to his brother.

So yeah, no prince for me.

Cyrus already sat at the table along with another man who only radiated a fraction of the power of the alpha. I didn't know if he was holding it back out of respect for Cyrus or if he just wasn't very powerful... which didn't make any sense. He had to be holding it back.

This was a dinner with the pack's betas and an alpha didn't pick weak betas.

The man had a similar build to Cyrus, big, bulky, and intimidating with a shaved head and piercing blue eyes, which only added to the theory that he was holding his power back. He couldn't look like an equal in power if he was also an equal physically. No alpha would allow that.

Beside him sat a beautiful woman radiating more power than the guy, and somehow, I could tell she was actually holding her power back. She wore a dress in the same style as mine, sleeveless, backless, and with fabric light and silky enough to show off every sleek curve and ripple of muscle. Hers was a deep green which brought out the gold in her eyes and the red accents in her light brown hair. It showed off her long neck and sculpted arms, and I'd bet if she stood, she'd have a six-pack and a great ass.

I was more or less fit — housecleaning could be hard work — but I didn't look nearly as good in the dress as she did and my nipples were still "at attention" with my constant, ever-so-slightly turned-on state. I would have been embarrassed about it if both of them hadn't looked at my face and forgotten to check out the rest of me.

Swell. Yep. I can't shift. Make your jokes now. Give me your disgusted looks. Bring it on.

Bishop cleared his throat and they jerked their attention away from me, but two more men and another woman strode into the room and took their seats. Now *they* stared at me.

Wonderful. I sat in the chair Bishop had pulled out for me, but that only made the man across from me raise his eyebrows in surprise.

"Knox's seat?" he asked, his attention jumping to Cyrus.

"Easier than adding an extra place setting," Bishop said, sitting in the chair beside me.

"Because bringing out silverware and an extra glass is a hardship," the new woman said. She wore a red version of my dress made from a material that was thicker than mine — thick enough that it might have better disguised my nipples — and had her dark hair piled on her head in an intricate updo.

With her attention on Bishop and only Bishop, she gracefully sat on the chair beside Green Dress. Her power wasn't particularly strong, and this time I clearly felt like she wasn't holding back, which shocked me. Maybe she wasn't a beta but a mate of one of the men.

Or maybe Cyrus wasn't like all the alphas I'd heard about and everything I knew about alphas and how to *be pack* was wrong.

"It's a waste to leave the spot empty every night," the leaner of the men Red Dress had entered with said. He sat beside her, his power similar in strength and also not suppressed, and offered me a warm, if confused smile, his attention on my face — most likely my black eyes.

"To answer the question you're all dying to ask," Cyrus said, drawing everyone's attention. "And I know it isn't 'will Knox be joining us for dinner' because you know he never does. This is Audrey. She'll be staying with us for a while," he said. "And yes, the rumors are true, she's the one we found injured in Darkweald."

"Rumors?" the other new man said with mock innocence as he took his place beside Lean Guy. He was older than the others with a hint of gray at his temples and deep laugh lines around his eyes.

He'd shown up in a black, lighter-material version of a kilt, his broad muscular chest and arms on full display. He wasn't as big as Cyrus or the man sitting across from me, but there was a sharpness to his features, a strong sense of feralness churning just under his skin that made him seem even more dangerous than Cyrus. A constant trickle of power radiated from him as if he was almost as strong as Cyrus or Bishop, was trying to fully contain it, but didn't have the same kind of control at suppressing it as the brothers did.

Cyrus rolled his eyes at him as if the man made

comments like that all the time, the sense of humor a strange juxtaposition to the sense of wildness radiating off him. "We all know Zavier said something before he and Lucius headed out."

"That boy just can't keep his mouth shut," the guy across from me said.

"Give the boy a break," Green Dress said with a laugh. "When was the last time the alpha's sons went out on patrol and came back with a woman?"

"Are we talking about all of them or just Bishop?" the older guy chuckled, making Red Dress shoot him a dirty look.

"And really, Cyrus," Green Dress continued, "if you wanted to keep things quiet, you shouldn't have asked to borrow a dress while I was in the middle of meeting with half of my staff."

Bishop threw his head back and laughed. "You went to Nova for a dress? Audrey was out for hours. There was plenty of time to send someone to get something."

Cyrus shot Bishop a dark look. "It is what it is. She didn't need clothes until she woke and we had no idea when that would be."

"You fell asleep in that chair after I checked on her," Green Dress said. "Didn't you?"

Cyrus huffed and Bishop turned to me, his eyes bright with amusement. "We'll get you some clothes tomorrow when I show you around town."

"You don't have to do that," I said. I was already in

their debt and still didn't believe that they wouldn't demand something in return.

"Better me than him," he said with a laugh, jerking his thumb at Cyrus. "He wouldn't know what looked good on a woman if it slapped him in the face."

The others at the table burst into laughter and the tension evaporated. Clearly that was an inside joke.

"I don't care if I look good. Just... more... covered," I murmured, my cheeks heating. "I'm not used to wearing something so..."

"Convenient to take off?" Green Dress said, making my thoughts jump to my achy need to seal the bond— hell, to just have sex with someone, anyone, my body didn't care who.

Everyone at the table stiffened ever-so-slightly and adjusted in their seats, suddenly uncomfortable, and I realized they'd just gotten a huge nose-full of my desire.

My cheeks burned hotter. Just great. You couldn't hide anything from a shifter. And while I'd known that, I hadn't really experienced it. Aside from school where only our teachers were shifters — and were probably used to smelling all kinds of things — Merrick had kept me more or less isolated from the rest of the pack. I'd been too busy for extra-curricular activities and only Mila had wanted to be my friend, and after I'd turned eighteen and my wolf hadn't woken, I'd been even more of an outcast.

Bishop cleared his throat and Cyrus's glower darkened while the older guy burst out laughing. The lean guy shot the older guy an exasperated look and pinched the bridge of his nose, while Red Dress's gaze fluttered up to Bishop with a heated look in her eyes then quickly looked away.

"That wasn't where I was going with that," Green Dress chuckled. "I meant given that you haven't shifted out the rest of your injuries, you probably aren't accustomed to shifting all the time."

"Is it really cold where you come from?" the exasperated man asked.

My embarrassment burned hotter, racing over my whole face and down my neck. "No. It's... complicated."

"And you're clearly not used to proper etiquette," Red Dressed huffed, her dark brown gaze flickering to Bishop again as if she couldn't keep her eyes off of him. And really, I couldn't blame her. Bishop was hot. Gorgeous and funny and kind. Who wouldn't want to be with him? "You don't release pheromones like that at the dinner table and if there's a risk of that happening you don't attend dinner."

"Lighten up, Velora," the older guy said. "She's young, she could be nearing her first heat and just hasn't figured out what the signs are or how to control it yet."

Oh. My. God! Did he really say that? Now my face was hotter than the sun. Yes, we shifters experienced periods where our sexual needs were stronger, usually in our late teens and early twenties, but it wasn't like a true heat like actual wolves.

"If that's the case then she shouldn't have come to dinner," Red Dress, Velora, said.

"She's our guest," Cyrus growled, letting a wave of power ripple over the table. Everyone's eyes jumped to him. "I told her to come. I wanted you to meet her so you don't accost her in the halls. Her reproductive cycle isn't your business—"

Green Dress raised an eyebrow at that, making Cyrus roll his eyes at her.

"Fine. Yes. If it's a problem, then it's yours, Nova, but only yours." He slid his glare over the others. "No, she's not accustomed to our ways. From the little she's told us, her pack is very different."

The guy who was exasperated with the older guy sat forward. "How different? Where do you come from? Are there actually any communities up north?"

I opened my mouth but I had no idea how to respond to that. Would they even believe me? Cyrus hadn't and had only accepted what I said as truth because of Whil.

"Very different," Bishop answered for me, "it's hard to explain, and she doesn't know."

His hand dipped under the table and settled on my knee, sending a ripple of calm through me as if he were my mate or a close friend and not someone I'd just met.

But that only reminded me of how shifters needed physical contact to help steady the animal aspect of their soul — even for those whose wolves were still asleep — and how I'd been without that kind of comfort since Mila had left. My reaction to Bishop's touch said I'd been without for so long anyone was good enough to steady my soul, even a stranger... albeit a kind stranger, but still a stranger.

Of course, the achy throbbing from the unsealed mating bond also didn't care he was a stranger or even my mate, and I gave the room another, mortifying, blast of my desire.

AUDREY

THE MUSCLES IN CYRUS'S JAW FLEXED AND HIS EYES GREW even darker, his wolf rising to the surface. Red Dress shot me a look of pure murder, while the older guy looked like he might cry from the effort of holding in his laughter.

"She'll be here for a while," Cyrus said, his voice clipped, "There'll be time to ask her questions later." His hard gaze slid to me. "But only if she wants to talk."

Oh, so now I have a choice?

"She's not a threat and may have to make Stonehaven her home," Cyrus continued.

"So, what you're really saying is let's pretend we're not assholes so we don't scare her away?" the older guy asked with a chuckle.

"Too late for that," the guy across from me said.

Cyrus glared at them, but the edges of his lips were quirked as if this was just the way dinners went with this group: light, fun, slightly dysfunctional like a good family, nothing at all like I'd seen with Merrick and his betas.

The thought made my chest squeeze, but I shoved the sensation back before it overwhelmed me. I had enough on my plate without being jealous of the *family* in front of me having dinner together

"So, the assholes around the table who we apparently trust with our lives are Finn—" Cyrus pointed to the guy sitting across from me. "He's the watch commander in Stonehaven, and Nova, the town's head physician." She was the woman in green who thought my reproductive cycle might actually be her business. "Beside her is Velora, who deals with all things administrative, Thane our chief of finance, and Deacon, our huntmaster in charge of the hunt teams." He was the older, mostly-naked guy, and he flashed me a warm, friendly smile. "Lucius, our primary advisor, is away on a diplomatic mission so you won't be able to meet him for a while."

After the introductions, the conversation thankfully turned away from me and who I was and where I was with my reproductive cycle and moved to lighter conversations about what was going on in town.

Two women brought out dinner as if we were in a restaurant, and I studied both of them, looking for signs of stress or fear, any indication that they were being treated badly, but it looked like they were content serving the alpha, his brother, and their betas.

I'd have to keep my eyes and ears open, but given how Bishop and Whil had treated me and how Cyrus's betas were even comfortable enough to tease him, I suspected what I saw was the truth. The people here were happy and Cyrus forcing me to tell him about the most embarrassing and shameful moment in my life was him being a protective alpha... like a good alpha was supposed to be.

Although could I really believe what I saw? I knew I wasn't a perfect judge of character, but I hadn't thought I was terrible. Except I hadn't seen being manipulated into starting the mating vows and almost sacrificed to a monster coming... although would anyone?

Regardless, I couldn't believe what I felt because I'd fallen for the fake fated mating call and I sure as hell hadn't thought that Royce would try to murder me.

The food was good and looked like food from home. I didn't know if that meant this realm was more or less the same as the mortal realm or not, but I was grateful I wouldn't have to adjust to blue goo or yellow sludge or something else unappealing.

Bishop's hand returned to my knee over and over again as the meal went on, a reassuring anchor as if he just knew his touch, even though we barely knew each other, would keep me calm. Not that I was going to run screaming from the room — where could I possibly go? — but my mind kept stuttering.

One moment I was fine, the next I remembered I was in another realm, I was mated to a man who didn't want me, I—

Bishop squeezed my knee and I refocused back on what Nova was saying.

"—early morning shift." She pushed her chair back, stood, and gave Cyrus a warm smile. There was a familiarity in it that spoke of a deep friendship and perhaps a little more. It made the hollowness in my chest swell, reminding me that I had a mate who hated me. "If you want to keep the rumors under wraps, I recommend not barging into my next meeting. Twice in as many days and people might start to think you've finally got your eyes on a mate."

Bishop choked on his wine and started coughing, his face turning red, making Nova quirk an eyebrow in curiosity. Velora shot me another withering look while Thane looked concerned, Finn angry, and Deacon like he'd just heard the best joke ever and was, for whatever ridiculous reason, trying not to laugh.

"Stop stirring trouble, Nova," Cyrus said. "It's been a stressful couple of days."

"So I can tease you tomorrow once you've recovered?" She batted her eyelashes at him in exaggerated innocence.

"Nova," he growled and she winked at me, her smile getting bigger.

"And you," she said to me, "should probably go to bed."

Her words spiked my desire again, and I became hyperaware of Bishop's hand on my thigh, the power radiating from his body, soft for now but I knew it could be hard and powerful in a second... and yeah, I was fully aware of the double meaning of that thought.

Finn groaned, and Velora huffed and left, while Thane pinched the bridge of his nose again, and Deacon roared with laughter, unable to hold it back any longer.

Embarrassment burned my face and neck, hell, my whole body, and if I'd thought Cyrus would have let me leave, I would have fled like Velora.

Cyrus released a sudden burst of power and I trembled with the need to kneel. Everyone's attention snapped to serious as if they hadn't expected that reaction.

"That was mean, Nova," Cyrus said.

"You're right. I'm sorry," she replied, her expression turning thoughtful as if Cyrus's reaction had made her reevaluate what she thought about me... or maybe him? Or had she purposely made that comment to figure out what Cyrus thought of me?

The idea was laughable. Even if I hadn't been mate bonded with his brother, he'd never be interested in me. It had to be obvious to everyone in the room I wasn't suppressing my power so they all knew I was weak, and Cyrus knew I couldn't shift. I wasn't mate material for an alpha or even the alpha's brother.

"What I mean," Nova said, all mischief gone from her expression, "is that you should shift out the rest of your injuries first *then* go to bed. And don't think shifting is enough. It just *looks* like enough. Even after you've gotten rid of what's left, your body is still processing the trauma you experienced. Needing two ampuls of elixir means a substantial amount of trauma. It's best to sleep it off." She shot Cyrus another strange look. "I'd have preferred her to have spent all day in bed like I prescribed." Then she turned back to me, her expression softening. "If you feel tired tomorrow, don't push through. Don't be a stubborn idiot like everyone else here at the table. Take a break."

"Right." I stood, taking that as my cue to leave. And even if it wasn't, I didn't want to stick around and risk any more comments that would embarrass me.

Bishop stood with me, and we left the dining room as Nova said something — too quietly for me to hear with my still-human hearing — and Cyrus growled in response.

"Nova certainly is something," I said once we were far enough away that they wouldn't hear me.

"Yes, she is," Bishop said with a brilliant heart-stopping grin, and I couldn't figure out if he was just impressed with her or attracted to her.

A sliver of jealousy oozed through me. I wanted to make Bishop smile like that, *and* I wanted to be as brave and bold as Nova. She teased her alpha, knowing it would piss him off and didn't care.

Of course, that also spoke to the type of man Cyrus was. He might not like Nova's ribbing but he still let her have her fun and be herself. He let all of his betas be themselves.

"She and Cyrus would have actually made a decent mating if she hadn't grown up with us like a sister."

"Her and Cyrus?" I burst out laughing. Surely that was a joke to lighten my mood. "I barely know either of them but I know he'd strangle her before they even got to the mating ceremony."

Bishop led me into the large front hall and we started up the grand staircase. "What you saw isn't exactly what it's like between them. He's worried about a lot of things right now, which worries Nova. He gets... well, like the way you saw him tonight and in Whil's cottage, and Nova digs in deeper with the teasing."

And one of those things he was worried about was me. "I really didn't mean to mate bond with Knox."

"I know you didn't." We stopped in front of my bedroom door, and Bishop hooked his finger under my chin, urging me to look up at him. His touch shivered through me and my desire burned stronger.

I resisted him, unable to look him in the eyes, knowing he could smell my arousal. God, why couldn't I keep it under control? But I knew why. He was kind and gorgeous, and feeling desire for him, hell even for the mate who didn't want me, was better than the icy hollowness threatening to consume me.

Except I was never going to let myself cross that line because I didn't know Bishop or any of these men and I was mated to his brother. If we couldn't break the bond, we'd either have to figure out another way to deal with it or accept it, and if it came down to accepting it, it would be less awkward if Bishop and I had never been intimate.

"I'm sorry about the—" My embarrassment burned hotter.

"It's not your fault." The pressure under my chin

increased and I gave in and looked up, falling into his stunning brown eyes and mesmerized by the brilliant flecks of green scattered through his irises.

He was so close I was fully wrapped in his bright, fresh-cut grass scent and could feel the heat from his body through the thin fabric of my dress. My mostly-hard nipples tightened all the way, and my desire heated, warming a little more of the icy hollowness... particularly the area between my thighs.

Now there was no doubt — if there'd been any before — that I wanted to have sex with Bishop.

"The mating bond wants to be sealed so it's increased your sexual desire," he said, his voice husky, teasing a shiver down my spine.

I knew that. Except my desire was supposed to be for my mate, not every hot guy around me.

His wolf's darkness flickered in his eyes but he kept his animal side buried. "The fact that you're so sensitive and the bond is only a few days old suggests it's strong."

"Or not normal," I replied, my voice breathy, my body aching. "That might make it easier to break." And that had to be the case because strong meant no hope, it meant always feeling Knox's hate for me and this aching need to be complete, and I didn't want to live feeling like this for the rest of my life.

Bishop glanced down, and I realized I'd placed my hand on his chest and was leaning in to him. The darkness in his eyes flickered again, and a hint of it stayed, turning the brown almost black and making the green flecks brighter. The soft power emanating from him grew stronger and his attention moved to my lips.

My pulse picked up. *Please kiss me.*

It wasn't as if I was in love with Knox.

Of course, I wasn't in love with Bishop, either.

He inhaled deeply, taking in my scent, and released a low rumble.

Yes, just lean forward. Kiss me.

Royce had stolen my first kiss but I ached to give Bishop my second... and third and fourth and—

With a soft, barely audible groan he squeezed his eyes shut and took a step back.

The icy hollowness swelled and my throat tightened.

He didn't want me. No one wanted me. I was weak and useless and—

No. I'm mated to his brother.

God, why was that so hard to remember?

But that was because Knox's rejection of our bond, even though it hadn't been intentional, magnified the hurt from all rejections.

"You should rest," Bishop said, his tone a little too bright. "Especially since you can't shift out the rest of your injuries. Come down for breakfast whenever you're ready and I'll show you around town."

"You really don't have to do that," I said, my voice still breathy even as the cold grew stronger.

If I hadn't been mated to his brother, he would have kissed me.

If I hadn't been mated to his brother, I wouldn't have wanted to throw myself at a complete stranger.

"You should probably keep helping Whil find a way to break this bond," I said, my chest tightening. My soul didn't want to break the bond even though it was the right thing to do. I didn't know Knox and it wasn't as if we were fated mates or anything. He was just the first person to touch me after I managed to escape that monster.

Remember that. Just keep remembering that.

"She has an apprentice who'll help her," Bishop said. "Tomorrow, I'm all yours."

Oh, how I wish you were.

He strode back to the grand staircase and I hurried into my room, my face on fire.

Mated to his brother. Mated to his brother. God damned mated to his brother.

AUDREY

THE RICH SCENT OF WOOD SMOKE WRAPPED AROUND ME and my eyes fluttered open. I lay on a soft bed of... I wasn't quite sure what. It looked like moss but felt more like bedding. Above me, two moons, one white and one slightly smaller and pink, were framed by tree branches heavy with leaves, and I realized I was in the small sacred grove outside the castle.

Except I had no idea how I'd gotten there.

Last thing I remembered, I'd gone to bed after that awkward dinner with Bishop, Cyrus, and their betas.

Now I was in their sacred grove... wearing my simple, white transformation dress.

This had to be a dream.

Something moved at the edge of my vision and I sat up, my pulse racing. Given what had happened the other night, I wouldn't have been surprised if that monster haunted my nightmares for the rest of my life.

But instead of the red-skinned monster, it was Bishop who stepped out of the shadows and into the circle of moonlight.

Except he didn't look right. He looked angry and hard, not the warm, gentle man who'd talked to me in Whil's greenhouse library. His hair partially hid his face, hanging forward and not braided back at the sides, and his eyes were dark and edged with a dangerous wildness.

He wore the practical pants that looked a little like cargo pants that he'd been wearing when I'd been awake, although these were black, not brown, but wasn't wearing his shirt, giving me an eye-full of his honed, muscular torso... or at least how I imagined his torso to look since this was a dream.

The breeze shifted, bringing with it more of the wood smoke scent and not Bishop's clean, fresh-cut grass scent, and the yearning within me swelled, overwhelming the icy hollowness.

This wasn't Bishop. This was my mate. His brother. And because I hadn't seen him in human form, my psyche had turned him into a more dangerous version of Bishop.

"I don't want you," he said, his voice low, his power rolling through me as he took a step toward me, his body belying his words.

But instead of making me bow in submission like it should have, it heated my insides, filling me with a tremendous, aching yearning. "I didn't mean to bond with you."

"Did you mean to bond with the man you said the vows to?" he growled, suddenly sounding angry that I'd wanted to bond with someone else.

"I thought he was my fated mate." My throat tightened and my cheeks burned, even as my desire grew stronger. "I thought we were destined for each other."

The words sounded ridiculous. How could I have possibly thought Royce was my destined mate when my real mate was standing right in front of me.

Except that wasn't true, either. Knox wasn't my real mate. He was just the man unfortunate enough to be caught up in the magic of my mating vows.

"No." The wild danger radiating from him grew stronger. "He's not your mate. I am."

"You're just saying that because this is a dream. You don't want me." He'd just said so, and he'd also made that perfectly clear in Whil's greenhouse library — if the constant aching cold of our rejected bond wasn't enough proof.

"No," he snarled. His canines extended and the look in his eyes turned ferocious, and even though he was still in his human form, I knew I wasn't talking to Knox the man anymore, but his wolf. "You're mine."

He closed the distance between us before I realized what was happening, grabbed a fistful of my hair, jerked my head back, and crashed his lips against mine in a savage, ravenous kiss.

The icy hollowness inside me shattered, and desperate

overwhelming need roared into every cell in my body and heaved at something powerful and wild deep within me. I needed him close, closer, needed him in me, needed to feel the bond between us empowered and alive. The bond just needed a spark, an electric magical jolt to bring it fully to life.

I tangled my fingers in his hair, digging my nails into his scalp, and kissed him back, that wildness hidden deep within me taking over and answering his hunger with its own.

With a snarl, he shoved me back, pinning me against a tree with his large powerful body.

"You. Are. Mine," he growled into my mouth, the words ringing within me like the gong of the fake mating call. "Mine forever."

"Yes," the wild something within me moaned.

I clung to him as he tore open the front of my transformation dress and roughly palmed my breast, still kissing me as if he were drowning and I was the only source of air. I wasn't going to think about how this was all a dream and how the gong of the fated mating call was merely an echo of what I'd experienced for real.

I ached to be desired, loved, accepted, and in this dream, the man who I'd accidentally forced a mating bond on was willing to give me all those things.

He roughly plucked and pinched my nipples, the pain building a need that was already threatening to consume me. Aching heat flooded my core, and moisture oozed down the inside of my thighs.

"Mine." He released my breast, palmed my mound, and shoved two fingers up inside me without warning.

I gasped at the sudden invasion, but my inner muscles fluttered with the promise of a release and my next breath came out on a low, desperate moan. My hips rolled, my body knowing what it wanted, but he yanked his fingers out instead of satisfying me and brought them to his lips.

A low growl rumbled in his chest, and he inhaled deeply, taking in my scent. My breath hitched at the sexual hunger in his eyes, and it stalled altogether as he sucked one finger clean then the other.

"Who is your mate?" he demanded.

"You are," I breathed.

"Say my name." He shoved his fingers back inside me and pressed his thumb against my clit but held it there, not rubbing the sensitive nub like I needed.

I rolled my hips again, but he pushed back, pinning my rear to the tree, holding me captive his hand in my hair controlling my head and his fingers inside me controlling my pelvis.

"Say. My. Name," he snarled.

"Knox." He jerked his fingers out and back in, the force jolting the breath from my lungs.

My inner muscles rippled again and my body trembled. I had no idea where in my subconscious this was coming from for me to dream this. Maybe it was because I knew how to make myself come with my fingers combined with how angry he was. Maybe I'd just spent too long fantasizing about what sex would actually be like.

He jerked his fingers out again and shoved them back in, snapping my attention back to him.

"Who am I?" he demanded.

"Knox," I moaned. "My mate."

"That's right." His fingers moved out and in faster and faster, his thrusts powerful, violent.

I clung to him. It was the only thing I could do captured between his hands and trapped against the tree, but I didn't feel helpless or in danger, not like I would if I'd been cornered by Sterling. No, I felt powerful. The icy hollowness was gone and a sun blazed within me, its heat and light reaching into every crack, every extremity, every cell of my body. My soul was alive with power and desire and that wildness that had been hidden within me until Knox had brought it out with his kiss and touch.

He pounded into me until I was wound so tight, burning with so much need, that it exploded out of me in a shattering, screaming rush. My inner muscles clamped down on his fingers with an orgasm more powerful than any I'd experienced before, stars flashed through my vision, and his expression turned smug and satisfied.

"You belong to me, and I will make him submit and claim you," he— no *his wolf* said as the stars faded and darkness consumed the grove.

AUDREY

I woke thrumming with a need more powerful than what I'd experienced so far, but still drowning in the ice of my frozen mating bond and confused as hell until I remembered it had all just been a dream.

Knox hadn't ripped an explosive orgasm from my body and hadn't claimed me as his. And I certainly hadn't heard the fated mating call ring in my soul. I didn't even know if that was what Knox really looked like. Hell, I didn't even want the bond with someone who didn't want me.

I shoved the covers aside, the fabric brushing against my hypersensitive skin, put my dress on — because that was all I had to wear, and I wasn't going to tempt fate by trying to race across the hall naked — and hurried to the bathroom to warm up and relieve the pressure in my core with my own fingers. If I scrubbed really well afterward, no one would be able to scent my arousal and as long as I didn't think about the dream — or anything else for that matter — I wouldn't end up embarrassing myself today.

Who was I kidding? I'd already embarrassed myself in front of everyone last night. Most of the pack's betas knew I was desperate for sex even if they didn't know it was because of a mating bond. Why not just share that with the rest of the town? Hell, the betas hadn't been sworn to secrecy about me, so the town probably knew already.

Maybe I could convince Bishop to skip the town tour and just stay in. We could go back to Whil's, and I could keep them supplied in tea or something while they searched for a way to break the mating bond.

Except the odds of breaking the bond were slim, and if Knox and I didn't seal it — which with him despising me was the likely scenario — I was going to be horny for the rest of my life.

Which was something I was just going to have to figure out how to deal with.

Maybe instead of going to Whil's we could just stay in my room and alleviate the sexual compulsion from the bond. It had been a bad idea last night and it still was this morning, but I was going to scream if I didn't have an orgasm and the one in my dream clearly hadn't been enough.

Besides, Knox didn't want me, so he shouldn't have a problem with me sleeping with his brother.

Except the thought of Knox going to some other woman to deal with the desire from the mating bond made me want to storm out of the bathroom, find him, and yell at him... even before he'd done anything.

And really, my reasons for not sleeping with Bishop hadn't changed.

Jeez. Dealing with my situation by myself was the only safe option.

Steam from the shower misted the mirror, indicating it was warm enough, and I hopped inside.

The water hit my sensitive skin and my core trembled in anticipation of coming even before I'd done anything. The memory of Knox kissing me like his life depended on it, all his ferocious power focused on me, not to make me submit but to turn me on, flooded me.

He could have made me kneel before him but he hadn't. Of course, that was because it was just a dream. From the ferocity and anger that had roared through the bond when he'd told me I wasn't his mate, I knew if anything happened between us, he'd demand my complete submission. He'd probably even claim me with his teeth.

The trembling in my core grew at the thought and I let myself fall into the fantasy. He'd want my submission, but he wouldn't hurt me. I'd be able to trust him because he was my mate.

If he was here in the shower, he'd turn me to face the spray and take me from behind. He'd push his cock into me while he arched me back, a hand on my neck to hold me in place and show me he was in control and the other between my thighs rubbing my clit.

I turned to face the spray just like in my fantasy, letting the water beat against my neck and chest. The water splattered against my thrumming body, tightening already taut nipples. In my fantasy, with my chest pushed out, they'd grow even more sensitive. Tingles would rush through me every time I drew a breath that would push them deeper into the spray, and my breath would get faster and faster.

Knox would pound his length into me over and over again just like he'd pounded his fingers into me in my dream, twisting me tight until stars flashed behind my lids again.

I pushed a finger inside me and rubbed my thumb against my clit. His breath would rush over the back of my neck and cheek and as he came inside me, his wolf would take over, extend his canines, and bite into the muscle between my neck and shoulder.

My inner muscles spasmed at the thought and tossed me over the edge. The orgasm wasn't as mind-blowing as the one in my dream, but it still left me trembling and breathless and satisfied — which had been the whole point of the exercise.

The throbbing need receded, once more overwhelmed by the icy hollowness, and I finished washing with a mix of bittersweet emotions. Sure, I wasn't going to lose my mind if I didn't have sex, but the emptiness wasn't much better than the need, just less embarrassing, and a part of me feared sex would never live up to the fantasy, even with someone as handsome — and likely experienced — as Bishop.

I pushed that thought aside. Thinking about Bishop and sex was a bad idea, especially since the Knox of my fantasies had had Bishop's face.

I dressed, finger-combed my hair so it wasn't a complete disaster, and went to the kitchen.

Bishop was waiting for me just like he'd promised. He sat at the kitchen table reading a book with two other books open in front of him. When he saw me, he flashed a heart-stopping smile and thankfully didn't sniff or make a face or say anything about my perpetual state of heightened arousal.

A selection of meat and fruit and pastries sat on the counter, the platters half empty as if a few someones had already taken their breakfast and left, and I filled up a plate and sat in the chair across from him.

The door leading to the garden was still open, and I could see the morning sunlight in the greenery beyond and smell the mix of fragrant herbs and flowers on the breeze.

"You ready for the grand tour?" he asked.

"Absolutely." I didn't know what was going to happen with the mating bond. If we couldn't sever it, I didn't know if I wanted to stay in the same town as Knox. Of course, I also didn't know if the bond would let me leave Knox. But if we could sever the bond and I did survive, perhaps this could be my new pack.

Bishop was kind and friendly, and Cyrus, while not

entirely friendly, didn't strike me as cruel — although I hadn't thought Royce was cruel, either. Their betas seemed to like and respect them, and I'd gotten a sense of genuine friendship among everyone at dinner last night. I was weak, and I might never be able to shift, but maybe they'd accept me like Bishop had said they would in Whil's cottage yesterday. Maybe there was a place where I belonged.

AUDREY

Once I'd finished breakfast, Bishop led me back to the grand staircase and out the front doors into a wide, open courtyard. An intricate bricked driveway — that may not have been an actual driveway in this world since I had no idea if they had cars here — led from the gate at the far end to the main steps of the house. It curled around a fountain with two enormous wolves on either side of a woman pouring water from a large urn and was edged with well-maintained gardens. Beyond stood the tall stone wall I'd seen yesterday and the stone buildings clustered together.

"This is the alpha's residence," Bishop said, turning and gesturing to the castle.

I turned with him, taking in the impressive structure with its grand front entrance and two distinct wings. Somewhere behind the large building was the kitchen's back door, the herb garden, private grove, and Whil's cottage. And looming above it all, stood a snow-topped mountain range as impressive as the mountains in Oregon.

Then Bishop led me beyond the wall protecting the alpha's residence into Old Town which was a collection of old stone buildings crowded close together creating a warren of alleys and nooks and small hidden gardens clustered within another stone wall that was thicker and higher than the wall around the alpha's residence.

It would have been gloomy and claustrophobic if it wasn't for the myriad flower boxes on window ledges and balconies blooming with a cacophony of colors.

Beyond Old Town lay New Town and as we walked down the main street leading away from Old Town's gate it was like traveling forward through time. The farther we walked, the wider the road grew and the newer the buildings looked. The side streets also grew wider, more like the streets I was used to, and while stone was still the predominant construction material, the blocks grew smaller and more precise in size like bricks. The brickwork also grew more fanciful with decorative ornamentations and there was more variety in the architectural styles.

There were more people in the newer part of town going about their business like it was a normal town, and if I didn't pay too much attention to the fact that there weren't any cars but hand-drawn carts and bicycles instead, I could pretend I was in any town in my realm. They had indoor plumbing and lights that seemed to work like in my realm, but with the town on the edge of the mountain with various slopes and stairs and winding paths, motorized vehicles weren't practical so the fact that I didn't see any cars didn't mean there weren't any in this realm.

Just like Nova and Velora, many of the women on the street wore the same backless dress I did and some of the men wore wraps like Deacon, suggesting that whatever their job was, they shifted frequently. But there were also people, both men and women, wearing clothes like Cyrus and Bishop did: pants and loose shirt which was a good sign that I'd be able to find something that covered more of me.

We wandered down to a large market on the edge of town, which I could hear from a few blocks away before we'd even rounded the corner of what looked to be a low, long warehouse. The market was filled with people talking and laughing and shopping. They were predominantly wolf shifters but there were humans and other shifters — who I could tell were shifters from their essence but not what kind — along with a few people with lizard-like features with human-like essences.

The space was packed with permanent and temporary stalls, tents, and horse-drawn carts, creating maze-like pathways almost as narrow as the "streets" in Old Town, and my nose was assaulted by a dizzying array of scents from various foods and wood smoke to people and animals.

"You're lucky you showed up in the summer," Bishop said. "The market isn't nearly as fun in the winter."

"This is incredible." I stopped at a permanent vendor's stall. It was a good-sized shed with a garage-style door that was opened all the way, revealing bins and shelves packed with books.

"A woman after my own heart," Bishop said, flashing me another one of those smiles that made my pulse skip. "Do you like to read?"

"A little." I hadn't had a lot of time to read. Merrick and Sterling had kept me busy cooking and cleaning for them, and I hadn't had a lot of money, since my cooking and cleaning were considered payment for living with them and my father had died with very little money and no property.

I ran my fingers over the spines in the closest bin but was unable to read any of the titles. "But it doesn't look like I'm going to be reading anything here," I added.

"I could borrow some primers from the school and teach you," he offered.

"That's still going to take a while, and I'm pretty sure you have better things to do with your time." Of course, if this realm was going to be my new home — and given that Cyrus hadn't initially believed I was from a different realm, indicating it didn't look good that Whil would be able to open a portal and send me home — I was going to need to learn things and being literate could help me find a job in this pack that didn't involve housecleaning. Except—

"If the books aren't in English, how are you speaking English?" I asked. There hadn't even been a moment with Cyrus where he spoke a different language then realized I didn't understand and switched.

"We're not," Bishop replied. "Well, you probably are. I asked Whil about that yesterday since you seemed to understand us right away."

"Let me guess. It has something to do with magic," I replied.

"Pretty much," Bishop said. "According to Whil all portals to our realm, permanent and temporary ones like the one you came through, have a sort of communication magic on them that enspells whoever passes through so they understand the language of whatever realm they're entering. But it's only for speech, which is why you can't read anything."

"Well, that's convenient." I picked up a colorful child's picture book and admired the art but still couldn't guess what was written beside the pictures.

"Your realm, along with a few others, and our realm used to be closely connected. The greater beings in our realm used to be worshiped as gods in the other realms."

"Used to be?" I put the picture book back and searched for a book for even younger children, one that might be like the reading primer Bishop had mentioned just to see if I could figure anything out.

"They might still be," he said. "But they haven't left our realm in a thousand years. A sleeping curse infected all of them, and the leaders of the other realms sealed off all the portals afraid that the curse would travel and infect the other realms."

"But if the portals were sealed, how did I get here?" I put the book back and looked at Bishop. "And if this realm has a sleeping curse on it, why is everyone still awake?"

"We're not entirely sure how you got here, although Whil has a theory," Bishop replied as we wandered away from the book vendor and headed to the next vendor over, a large red tent with a swirling gold pattern on it. "And only the greater beings were affected by the curse. But the leaders in the other realms didn't know that at the time and now Whil has no way of telling them that it's safe to reopen the portals."

"So Whil has been unable to return to Faerie for a thousand years?" And given that I hadn't seen any other fae it was probably a good guess that there weren't other fae here, or fae she was close to.

Was she homesick? Would I become homesick even though I had no one to return to?

I didn't think so. Sure, I'd miss Mila, but she had a mate and was happy, and being here was a lot better than being there.

I drew in a deep breath, savoring all the competing scents. I still wasn't certain about Bishop and Cyrus, and I certainly wasn't certain about my unwanted mate, but I still felt freer than I ever had before.

With a skip in my step, I hurried to the red tent and reached to pull back the flap.

"Ah, Audrey," Bishop said, "You might want—"

I stepped through the flap and froze. It was filled with lingerie of all shapes and sizes and colors in silky fabrics and see-through fabric and—

Desire surged through me, making the young woman minding the tent sniff and give me a knowing smile.

"Not this one," I said, turning and trying to push Bishop back before he could enter, my face on fire.

"You sure?" he said, his eyes bright with mischief. "Every woman needs a few nice things to make her feel sexy."

"Feeling sexy isn't my problem." Or at least, feeling like I needed sex wasn't. "Besides, what would I do with them? I'm trying to get rid of a mate, not win one," I whispered, praying I was only loud enough for Bishop to hear.

"But not forever," he whispered back.

AUDREY

"You're safe here and you're allowed to make plans for the future," Bishop added, his voice soft and filled with a gentleness that made me want to burrow against him and never leave the comfort of his touch.

Instead, I pressed my palms against his chest to urge him to step back onto the street, but my thoughts stalled at the feel of all that powerful muscle hidden underneath his shirt then jumped to last night's dream and how I'd imagined what all that muscle had looked like and felt like and—

Bishop's wolf darkened his eyes and his nostrils flared, taking in my scent.

"I can't make plans. Not really," I forced out, my voice breathy. "There's almost no chance Whil will be able to break the mating bond and I'm certain lingerie won't change—" I glanced back at the shop attendant who was eagerly watching us. "It won't change *his* mind about me."

"So don't buy it for him." His gaze flickered to my lips as if he was thinking of kissing me and my need flared stronger. "Buy it for yourself. Let yourself feel beautiful."

I slid my hands up his chest, raised up on my toes, and tilted my head up in invitation. *Please kiss me.* Making myself come in the shower hadn't been nearly enough. Of course, having sex with Bishop wouldn't satisfy my need, either. The only one who could was Knox and he didn't want me.

The icy hollowness enveloped some of my desire, and my throat tightened with the grief of rejection that I didn't want but couldn't stop feeling because of the damned mating bond.

The desire in Bishop's eyes shifted to worry, as he clearly saw my change of thoughts. "However this works out, it will be okay. I'll keep you safe. I promise."

Except he couldn't promise that and there wasn't anything he or I or anyone could do about it.

So move on. Move forward. It's the only thing I can do.

I forced a smile and stepped back. "I'm pretty sure I asked for clothes that involved more material, not less."

His worry blossomed into a heart-stopping smile. "You're right. As my lady wishes."

We left the lingerie store and slowly wandered around the market, Bishop letting me explore everything at my own pace, not just the clothing stores. People smiled, waved, and chatted with him while I shopped, but I never felt like he was ignoring me. It was clear the pack loved him, just like it had been clear last night that the betas loved him and Cyrus, and a part of me was grateful he was drawing their attention away from me and my bruised face... after, of course, they all stared at me.

By late morning, Bishop carried two bags full of clothes and another with a practical pair of hiking boots.

It was too much. I could have gotten by with a shirt, a pair of pants, and the boots, but Bishop kept adding things when we went to pay. He even added a pink version of the dress I was wearing when he thought I wasn't looking even though I'd stressed practical clothes only.

A part of me heated at the idea that he wanted to see me in a dress again even though I'd already nixed the idea of lingerie. But just because I'd said no, didn't mean I could stop my mind from imagining the fantasy of him releasing the two simple ties and letting the silky fabric slide off my body.

Now I sat in a small park with benches, picnic tables, and a playground for the children while Bishop got us lunch.

Children ran around laughing and yelling one third fully clothed, another third completely naked, and the final third as wolf pups.

Their joy was infectious and I couldn't help smiling, but it was a bittersweet smile. If our pack hadn't paid that witch all those years ago to prevent us from shifting until we were eighteen this was what our playgrounds would have looked like. Shifters being themselves, free from the moment they were born. They wouldn't have been able to shift until at least five or six years old but they'd still have been connected with the wolf half of their soul from the moment they were born.

Two of the pups started wrestling and a woman at a picnic table called out to them, but they ignored her. Another woman nearby laughed and said something, and the first woman chuckled with her. Then the first woman stood, slipped out of her dress, shifted, and bounded over to them.

It was so natural it took me a moment to realize I hadn't been shocked at her being naked. She was a mom with her kids and was stopping a fight before it got serious. She'd just so happened to strip and shift to do it.

I turned away before my bittersweet joy at watching the kids play turned completely sour.

My childhood had been what it had been and I was what I was. I couldn't change it or me no matter what I wanted, and I wasn't going to let Knox's rejection of our mating bond make me feel sorry for myself about that.

I'd decided I was done with that in the lingerie tent, and I was going to stick with that decision.

Still, I wasn't sure I could keep watching the family and life I hadn't had so I let my gaze wander over the rest of the area instead of the playground.

The park sat at the edge of town on the far side of the market. A dozen large old trees delineated two of its sides from the rest of the market, but the third and fourth sides were wide open. The grass had been cut to the edge of the park but not beyond and was the only thing indicating where the park stopped and the rolling grassy foothills began.

Beyond stretched a breathtaking vista, and if I didn't look up at the ghosts of the two moons, I could almost pretend I was close to home in the mortal realm. Green and yellow grass speckled with flowers waved in a gentle breeze, white clouds scuttled across a brilliant blue sky, and the yellow sun warmed my skin.

One of the larger clouds drifted over the sun, and the wind gusted, making the grass ripple and undulate like water. The bigger movement accentuated a break in the ripple as if the grass were parting around something.

Probably a rock. We were in the foothills after all.

But the cloud scuttled away with another gust and the bright sunlight seemed to shine a spotlight on something black within the grass that wasn't a rock. Probably a shifter. Whoever it was wasn't big enough to be a full-sized wolf but could have been a kid or teen. He or she was probably honing their stalking skills, and while it seemed strange to me to see a youth hunting, just like the pups playing on the playground, it was probably common here.

A dozen feet away I caught glimpses of two more black shapes slinking through the grass together. They drew closer to the edge of the long stalks and I couldn't tell if they were practicing hunting as a pack or if the two of them were hunting the single wolf.

Then the solo wolf lifted his head and howled,

revealing that he wasn't a wolf but a dog with a wide, square head and short black fur.

Dozens of howls responded and the two wolves— no dogs, the dogs that had been at the edge of the grass, raced into the park. They attacked a woman, wrenching her to the ground and killing her before I had time to call out.

The park erupted into chaos, people screaming and running, grabbing children and leaving their shopping and lunches.

More dogs barreled out from between the stalls and tents onto the street. Even though they looked like dogs, they attacked like big cats, pouncing and clawing as well as biting and tearing into people who weren't fast enough to defend themselves or flee. Men and women shifted, not bothering to undress, sacrificing their clothes to the magic that made them shifters, while others stayed human but grew claws.

A wolf lunged at another dog-creature coming out of the tall grass. It tried to get on top and bite the dog's neck or claw open its belly. But the wolf could barely catch it and when it did, it couldn't sink its teeth or claws into the dog's hide.

I scrambled from the picnic table, abandoning my new clothes, and raced into the market's maze-like streets away from the chaos.

The crowd jostled me, too many people trying to squeeze through the narrow space at the same time. Ahead of me, a man with a wailing toddler bumped a small girl, knocking her down, but didn't even glance at her. He probably didn't even know he'd run into her.

I grabbed her arm and hauled her to her feet. She gasped a thank you and we turned to keep going, but a desperate scream, somewhere ahead of us, stopped us in our tracks. The crowd heaved, people pushing and scrambling to change directions.

"This way," the girl said, yanking me back a few steps to a narrow space between two permanent sheds.

With her small stature, she easily slipped inside and quickly headed toward the band of sunlight on the other side. I hesitated for a second. I was bigger than her and it was going to be a tight fit. I didn't want to risk getting stuck... except if it was a tight fit for me, it would be an impossible fit for the dogs.

Oh, this is a bad idea.

I shoved myself inside, needing to exhale and take little gasping breaths to fit. The girl had already vanished out the other end and all that lay ahead of me was the narrow strip of sunlight.

Behind me, I heard the crowd race past, then the dogs. Someone screamed, the sound desperate and filled with agony, and the breeze gusted past me filled with the metallic tang of blood and something dark and foul that could only have been from the dogs.

I shoved my way forward, the rough wooden walls pinning me in, catching on my dress and scratching my bare skin. My heart pounded and fear twisted my gut into a frozen knot. I couldn't turn my head to look behind me and had no way of knowing if any of the dogs had noticed me.

Then wild, ferocious barking roared behind me followed by heavy violent banging that shook the sheds.

My heart jerked into overdrive. At least one of the dogs had noticed me and was trying to break through the sheds.

I strained to shuffle faster, desperate to get to the ever-growing band of light at the end.

The dog howled and snarled and the sheds shuddered again. Wood cracked and crunched, the sound shooting ice through me and the foul scent swept around me as hot breath hit my bare arm.

Oh, God. It was right behind me and I couldn't even turn to face it... and I had no idea if not being able to see my death coming was the better option or not.

The end of the sheds drew closer as it snarled and crashed into the sheds again. More wood crunched and something wet grazed my elbow.

Shit shit shit.

I heaved myself sideways in a desperate, awkward dive for safety and toppled out the other side, crashing onto the cobbled street. The dog smashed through the rest of the sheds and bounded toward me, and I scrambled to my feet, but there was no way I'd be able to outrun the thing.

Then two gray wolves leaped on it, clawing and biting and trying to pin it to the ground.

Run, a male voice barked. It sounded a lot like Finn

and was backed with a wave of power that had me racing away from them and the heart of the market before I fully knew what I was doing.

The foul smell from the dogs and the cloying reek of blood choked me. All around me people screamed, children wailed, dogs barked, and wolves howled. A part of me howled at the fact that running was the only thing I could do. I couldn't shift and even if I could, I didn't know how to fight. I didn't even know if it was possible for a wolf to take down one of the dog-monsters.

I raced around a corner into a small, recessed area and stumbled to a halt. A dog had cornered a group of children and — from the two medium-sized bodies laying a few feet away from the trembling group — had already killed two of them.

A scrawny boy, probably about twelve, held a wailing toddler, while two little girls cowered behind him, one sobbing, the other deathly pale and silent. A slightly larger boy who looked to be about the same age as the other one stood in front of them, snarling at the dog with his canines and claws extended.

There were only two ways out of the area, the narrow path I'd run out of and a wider path big enough for the shattered vegetable cart lying a few feet away. But neither was an option. The dog had the kids backed into a corner between two shallow vendor stalls — also filled with produce and nothing that could be used as an effective weapon — and the stalls stood in front of a tall wall that didn't have any windows.

The only way the kids were going to get away was if something distracted the dog, and with no one else around, that something had to be me. No way was I going to leave these children to their fate, no matter how stupid it was to draw the dog's attention.

AUDREY

"Hey!" I yelled at the dog, keeping close to the path behind me so I could make a run for it and have as much of a head start as possible.

The dog swung its large, blocky head at me and snarled, and the sobbing girl leaped away from the group in the direction of the larger opening. But the dog jerked his head back to them and lunged at the girl.

The boy defending them grabbed her arm and shoved her behind him as he dove to meet the dog's attack. My pulse stalled. It was a suicidal move, and I didn't need my imagination to know the boy was going to be ripped to shreds like the two other kids already on the ground.

I grabbed a piece of the broken cart roughly the size of a baseball bat and barreled at the dog, screaming.

The creature batted the boy aside, its claws tearing into his back, and leaped at me.

Oh fuck oh fuck oh fuck.

I heaved to the side, somehow avoiding its claws, and bashed the dog over the head. The strike didn't even make it hesitate. With a roar, it lunged at me and I ran, praying it would follow.

It did but caught up quickly and rammed its blocky head into me, shoving me forward. I hit the ground, losing my makeshift club, caught a glimpse of darkness out of the corner of my eye, and threw myself to the side.

The dog's claws tore through my dress and into the cobblestones, and I rolled away, narrowly avoiding another swipe.

My elbow hit my club and I grabbed it and swung with all my might. It broke over the dog's head, stunning it long enough for me to scramble to my feet and yell at the kids.

"Run!" I screamed at them. A pressure of something thud-thudded in my chest and all of the kids bolted.

The dog turned to go after them, and I threw myself at it, ramming my shoulder against its side and only managing to redirect its attention.

Yep, I was going to die.

At least I was going to do it saving a bunch of kids and not being eaten by a monster to give the assholes Sterling and Royce more power.

The dog snapped at me, its teeth grazing my arm, and I stumbled back, lost my balance, and fell.

Thankfully the kids ran. The pale-faced girl tripped and the bigger of the two boys picked her up and slung her over his shoulder with his supernatural strength. His dark gaze met mine for a second, his expression filled with fear, but he knew what he had to do, and that wasn't to save me. It was to save the younger kids.

The dog snapped and swiped at me and I rolled out of the way again. A flicker of pain grazed across my back and I tried to scramble to my feet, but the dog rammed me with its head and knocked me back down right into the corner the kids had been in.

Shit.

With a snarl, the dog dove in to bite me, but a huge black wolf bounded out of nowhere and tackled it.

They rolled across the blood-slicked cobblestone, biting and clawing and snarling, their bodies twisting and heaving in a violent struggle.

I staggered to my feet, knowing I needed to get the hell out of there. If the wolf didn't win, I was as good as dead.

But before I could run, the wolf snapped its teeth on the dog's throat and tore open its flesh.

The dog collapsed, its blood gushing around it and the wolf, and I clutched the edge of the stall beside me, my pulse still pounding and my body trembling.

"Thank God," I gasped. *Oh, thank God.*

The wolf raised his head, capturing me with piercing, black eyes flecked with green, and everything within me froze.

Knox.

I didn't know his wolf form well enough to recognize

him, but I knew in my soul the wolf in front of me was Knox.

Knox had saved me.

My whole being strained toward him, my soul aching with the bond he refused to accept.

Blood dripped from his snout as he stared at me, no growling, no angry words, nothing. It was like everything, all thought and sound, even the air, had been sucked from around us and we were suspended in this moment.

Him and me.

Bound together with a bond neither of us wanted. Forever. Trapped by our circumstances.

The icy hollowness inside me remained cold, his rejection still strong, but it didn't grow, didn't threaten to bring me to my knees with emotions I didn't want and couldn't control.

"What the fuck!" Cyrus roared from down the wider road, shattering the moment.

The world rushed back to life around me, people yelling, but not screaming, the foul reek of the dogs and the metallic bite of blood, but also the seductive wood smoke scent that my soul insisted belonged to me.

Knox raced away, neither brother acknowledging the other — although they could have communicated tele-pathically and just not included me in the conversation — and Cyrus stormed toward me.

He was breathtaking and terrifying and completely naked, revealing every powerful, dangerous inch of his body. His eyes were black with his wolf, his canines and claws extended, and blood streaked across his chest indicating that while he'd fought in wolf form — since he was naked — he'd also just been fighting in his human form, too.

Unable to stop myself, my gaze followed the streak of blood on his chest down to his partially erect cock, and my breath stalled. He was bigger than I expected, certainly bigger than the glimpse I'd gotten of Sterling all those years ago.

The throbbing need inside me surged, and all I could think about was how would it feel to have all that dangerous power holding me, pushing into me, driving me crazy.

"Don't you ever pick a fight with a grimalkin again." His power rolled off him in a great wave with his fury.

I jerked my attention up and met his glare while clinging to the edge of the vegetable stall to keep standing. I would *not* submit to him. Not when I knew what I'd done was right.

"I don't care how noble the cause or how many children you think you can save. You'll never do that again."

"You're not my alpha," I snarled back, even though the smart thing would be to submit and keep my mouth shut. But I'd just run for my life again and had been helpless *again*. I was furious to the point of tears that I was useless, that the only thing I was good for was being a sacrifice, even if this time it had been my choice. There was more to me than that. There had to be.

"You're mated to my brother," he growled. "That

makes me your alpha and I'm giving you a direct order. Do I need to make you submit to acknowledge it?"

More power rolled off him and I clutched the stall, refusing to give in. "I wasn't going to let that— that whatever it was kill them." And now that I thought about it, that dog, or rather, grimalkin, could have easily killed them. It had played with them first, picking them off one at a time and building up their fear, and would have continued to do so if I hadn't stepped in.

"It almost killed you," he said as he stepped close, using his size to intimidate me — and with all his muscle and towering above me, he sure as hell was intimidating. He trembled, a low, dangerous growl rumbling in his chest, and anger blazed in his eyes along with— was that fear? "Your death hurts my brother."

It was fear. Just not fear for me.

"My death will solve his problem." I strained my neck to maintain eye contact in a direct challenge. I didn't care if he punished me over this. I'd been punished for everything else. This at least was worth it. "I will *never* abandon a child."

If I could help it, no child would ever suffer like I had. Those kids had needed someone to protect them and I was there. It was that simple. It didn't matter if I could have won the fight or not. Someone had needed to do something.

Something plopped on the ground by my foot, the sound wet and heavy, and Cyrus stepped back and looked down, breaking eye contact first and drawing my attention down as well.

I stood in a small puddle of blood. Of course I was. I was probably covered in blood with all the rolling around I'd done fighting the grimalkin. Hell, who was I kidding? I'd been running for my life there hadn't been any fighting involved.

But there was something else important about the pool at my feet...

Except with the adrenaline rushing from my body, I couldn't make my mind focus enough to figure it out.

There was blood all over the area, pools by the bodies of the two dead kids and by the dead grimalkin, but here...?

"Fuck," Cyrus snarled and he jerked forward as my legs gave out and the world went black.

CYRUS

I CAUGHT AUDREY AS SHE PASSED OUT, HEFTED HER INTO my arms, and marched down the street to where Nova had set up her medical team.

Damn this woman.

I'd seen the kids run past and Audrey fighting the grimalkin and knew exactly what had happened since I already knew she knew how to run away. She'd chosen to stay and sacrifice herself to distract the grimalkin so the kids could escape.

And if it hadn't been the stupidest thing she could have possibly done, I would have been thrilled to learn that Knox's unwanted mate was willing to risk her life to save children.

But she'd known she hadn't stood a chance and knew that breaking the bond by dying could break Knox's spirit, and she'd made the choice anyway. And while she had no idea that Knox could go feral if their bond suddenly shattered, it still made me furious that she'd choose suicide by grimalkin to solve her problems... even if it was to save children.

Fuck.

Knox would have made the same choice without giving it a second thought.

So would I or Bishop.

And as much as I really didn't want to admit it, the glimpse I'd gotten from her before Knox had leaped in and killed the grimalkin, had been breathtaking. Even with her dress torn and her face bruised and body scratched, she'd been stunning.

She'd radiated a determination and ferociousness that told me exactly how she'd survived the attack that had left her almost dead in Darkweald.

I had no doubt that there was a wolf inside her. I just didn't know how to break her curse and let it out. Even if that wolf wasn't powerful, she was going to be magnificent. She'd be a fierce mother and when she found her confidence, like I'd seen tiny glimpses of at dinner last night, she'd be a dazzling mate.

Knox was a fucking moron for not giving her a chance.

And now she was in my arms with her blood oozing down my bare chest while my partial hard-on from just holding her was getting harder by the second, despite my worry about how much blood she was losing.

I was never going to hear the end of it.

There was no way Nova wouldn't notice I was turned

on and she'd jump to the correct conclusion that Audrey was the cause.

Nova's team was in the large square at the edge of the market by the main road, a wide open space with a fountain that allowed for easy access to the hospital for the most seriously injured, as well as a place to treat those not as injured or who couldn't be moved without first aid first.

Doctors, nurses, and medics rushed to save lives, and civilians helped out by cleaning minor scrapes and applying pressure to more serious injuries until someone could help. Nova stood at the front of the chaos doing triage and directing people to various sides of the square.

It always shocked me a little to see her so serious, even though we'd grown up together in the alpha's residence, and I knew she was an exceptional doctor and leader. To me, she'd always be the bratty little almost-sister who used to leave frogs in my bed or get up in the middle of the night and change my alarm clock so I'd be late for school.

She turned and saw me holding a bleeding Audrey and sporting a raging hard-on and rushed down the street to meet us.

"How bad?" she asked all business, but I knew the second Audrey was safe and Nova had time to catch her breath she was going to bring up the whole mate conversation that she'd brought up at dinner.

"I didn't get a chance to get a good look, but we have to treat it like it's serious."

Her lips twitched.

Here it came.

Except her attention dipped to Audrey's face and her still obvious bruises and serious-Nova returned. "Why didn't she shift before bed like I told her to?"

"Because she can't," I said. It wasn't my place to share that particular detail, but Nova needed to know to treat her properly. "I don't know if she even heals like a shifter. You have to treat her like she's human."

"Are you sure?" she asked, hurrying us to the right-hand side of the square where there were more people and supplies, not to mention more people scrambling to save lives.

"Whil has already confirmed it."

"Well, shit. Practically no essence and can't even shift." She caught the attention of a nearby medic and indicated he needed to take over triage then grabbed a blanket from a cart of blankets and set it on the ground near a packed medic's bag and a lineup of supplies ready to be used.

I laid Audrey facedown, her cheek on the blanket, and knelt beside her, concern finally weakening my hard-on. Blood smeared her back, oozing from four gashes, and trickled down her ribs. She was going to have more scars to add to the still bright red scars from all the wounds she had when we found her.

"I hate to say it, because she was really sweet at dinner last night," Nova said, pulling on a pair of gloves and laying two thick pieces of gauze on half of Audrey's wound, "but you can't take her as your mate. No one will accept her as an alpha."

She directed my hands to the gauze and I applied pressure. "I'm not interested in mating her."

Nova shot my cock a quick look, quirked an eyebrow then grabbed a bottle of saline and went to work. "I've never seen you react this way to a woman."

Which was true and scared the shit out of me. If it had been any other woman, I would have already handed her over to someone else and sought out Bishop, Finn, and Deacon to deal with this attack, but I hadn't. I'd personally carried her to Nova. And while I could lie and say I'd needed to be there in person to tell Nova that Audrey couldn't shift, I could have easily passed that information on to whoever I'd handed her off to and Nova knew that.

I could lie to myself and say I was protecting Knox, but that wasn't entirely true. There was something about Audrey, something that made me angry and protective and on-edge in a way I'd never been before.

Except there was still a chance we couldn't trust her and Knox was potentially stuck with her for the rest of his life and without a doubt, Bishop was sweet on her.

For the sake of the pack, I had to keep my head on straight.

But seeing her fight that grimalkin along with feeling her resist my power while refusing to break eye contact and submit to tell me she'd always sacrifice herself to protect children had made my wolf sit up and take notice in a way he'd never noticed another female before and—

Head on straight, for fuck's sake.

"She's been through hell and she's alone here, Nova," I ground out, as Nova put two new pieces of gauze on the wounds she just cleaned and redirected my hands.

And Audrey's hell had been worse than I'd imagined. After dinner, Bishop had joined me in my office and filled me in on what he'd learned about Audrey while they were at Whil's. She'd been told her whole life she was worthless because her essence was so weak and she'd been afraid for a long time, which Bishop assumed meant she'd been abused when she was younger.

The fact that she'd fought that grimalkin to save those kids and then yelled at me about never abandoning a child just added to Bishop's assumption about how she'd grown up.

"She needs people on her side," I finished. "That's it."

Now it was Nova's turn to roll her eyes at me. "Sure it is."

"There are more important things to worry about right now."

"Yes, and you being attracted to her is a problem," Nova said.

Fuck, I need to get out of this conversation without making Nova even more suspicious.

"I'm attracted to a lot of women," I huffed, trying to sound indifferent.

But my words only made Nova narrow her eyes at me,

reminding me that I was a fucking idiot if I was going to get anything past her.

It was like I was eight again thinking I could lie to her and she'd buy it. She'd never bought it and I never learned because a part of me wanted her to call me out on it, needed her to. She, like Bishop and Knox, kept me honest with myself.

"Bishop is attracted to anything with a uterus. You're not," she said, cracking the seal on an ampule of healing elixir and dribbling the liquid into Audrey's mouth. "It sucks in a lot of ways. But you have to do what's right for the pack."

"I'm not the alpha's only son," I growled. I hated that Nova was right, hated that whether I wanted Audrey to be my mate or not, I didn't have a choice.

"Knox will never accept leading the pack and Bishop would need one hell of a woman to make the hard decisions and demand submission when necessary. That or share the alpha mating with another man or woman," she said, motioning to Harris, her second-in-command, to come over. "And we both know the only people he'd share a mate with is you and Knox."

Harris handed a bag of supplies to someone else and hurried to Nova's side.

"Stitch her up," she ordered as she stood and peeled off her gloves. "It's not as bad as it looks but with her essence so weak, I don't want to take any chances."

"Not bad? She's unconscious." And I was painted in

too much blood, not to mention the gauze beneath my hands was red and wet.

"She passed out because she overexerted herself and is still recovering from her previous injuries." Nova's expression softened.

Yeah, she could see right through me. I'd spent a dinner with Audrey, that was it, and I was already more attracted to her than any other woman in the pack. What a fucking mess.

Another medic came up beside me and took over applying pressure to her wounds, and I forced myself to move away from her.

She wasn't mine. She was Knox's or maybe Bishop's if the bond could be broken, and she was going to be fine. I had more important things to worry about, like figuring out how those grimalkins got so close to town and why there were so many of them.

AUDREY

ONCE AGAIN, I WAS ENVELOPED IN THE RICH, COMFORTING scent of wood smoke and my eyes fluttered open to see Knox, or rather dream-Knox, storm toward me from the shadows and into the moonlight bathing the sacred grove beside the alpha's castle.

Power rolled off him, igniting my desire instead of demanding submission just like the last time I'd had this dream, and my core clenched in anticipation. It didn't matter that he looked furious, ready to tear me apart. I burned for him, for all that ferocity pounding into me... even if this was just a dream.

"You fought that grimalkin," he snarled.

Swell. Dream-Knox was going to yell at me like Cyrus had.

I started to rise. No way was I going to face him sitting on the ground, but he pounced on me, capturing my face between his large hands and kissing me with the same wild passion as before.

He pushed me back to my knees, grabbed my hair, and deepened the kiss. His tongue invaded my mouth, possessing me, stealing my breath, and making the need from our mating bond turn to molten desire between my thighs.

"You fought that grimalkin," he growled into my mouth. "I knew you were a fighter." He pulled back just enough for his dark wolf's eyes to capture me, his gaze boring into me as if he could see my soul—

No, my wolf. It was as if he could see my wolf.

"I knew the second your soul reached into mine you were my mate. Determined, ferocious, powerful."

A flicker of ice from human-Knox's rejection sliced into my need, reminding me that this wasn't real. "I'm not powerful. I'm—"

"You're a fucking goddess," he said. "You just need to wake up."

But if I woke, this dream would end and I didn't want it to end.

"I *will* make him see the truth," Knox's wolf said. "You're mine. You've always been mine and you'll always be mine."

The gong of a fated mating call reverberated through me, just like in the dream last night, and I tangled my fingers in his hair and smashed my lips against his. I wanted to believe that mate bonding with him hadn't been a mistake, that it had been fate, and he was as much mine as I was his.

And for this dream, he was.

The wild thing inside me, my dream-wolf waiting to be woken, flooded my veins, igniting the cells in my body. Power rolled off me, crashing against Knox's, shooting sparks around us. It *thu-thudded* in my heart, and another resounding gong boomed, ringing in my ears, my body, my soul.

"Mine." His grip in my hair tightened and he slipped his hand beneath my skirt and shoved two fingers into my soaking wet core.

I gasped and he pushed his tongue deeper into my mouth, wild, hungry, unable to get enough. His need sang through our bond as aching and desperate as mine, connecting us in a way that should have terrified me, but didn't because this was a dream.

Except there was also a painful edge to his need, a tremendous fear from human-Knox that wolf-Knox was determined to conquer.

He pounded his fingers into me while his lips on my mouth and his hand in my hair held me captive unable to do anything but submit to the pleasure. The impacts jolted the breath from my lungs and shot snaps of hot-white need through me that added to my desire slicking his fingers.

"Who do you belong to?" he snarled.

"You," I gasped.

"Who?" He ground his thumb against my clit and the snaps turned into a blazing, twisting inferno.

"You, Knox," I moaned as the gong sounded again. It boomed through every cell of my body and erupted in my core. My muscles clenched tight around his fingers, but he kept pounding, drawing the orgasm out into ragged, shuddering pleasure.

Stars flashed across my vision again and my breath came in short sharp gasps. I sagged in his arms, but he didn't give me time to recover. He flipped me over, grabbed my hips, and pushed his thick cock into my entrance.

A long, ragged groan escaped my lips, the sensation of him filling me, stretching me, overloading my senses.

In the back of my mind, I knew it would feel different when I did this for real... although maybe not. I was so wet, so boneless from my first orgasm, that I might be able to take him without pain.

"You," he said, his voice low and dangerous, making my core flutter as if I hadn't just come. "You are my goddess."

He withdrew and pushed back in, again and again, pulling my hips back to meet his thrusts, our skin slapping together, our breaths bursting from our bodies with each ferocious, delicious impact.

Pleasure spun me tighter and tighter and I couldn't catch my breath or get my bearings. There was only Knox and his cock hitting an amazing spot inside me and our bond blazing with heat and light and power around my heart.

With a snarl, he grabbed my throat and urged me to sit up, capturing me against his powerful, muscular chest while his other hand went to my clit, his fingers hitting the sensitive nub and shooting another small orgasm through me.

"Oh, God," I said, my body shuddering at his savage, mind-blowing assault.

"More," he growled, his fingers furiously rubbing my clit, taking that small orgasm and exploding it into spinning, screaming, shattering release.

More stars— no, fireworks tore through me as Knox clamped his canines in my shoulder and came. His cock swelled and his hot cum surged inside me.

He clung to me, buried to the hilt, his tense body wrapped around me and his teeth in my flesh.

Aftershocks rippled through me, over and over again, and I sagged into his embrace, boneless and overflowing with the most amazing sensation.

His canines slowly shrank back to human-size, but he kept his lips pressed against my shoulder.

"I need you, Audrey," he murmured, his lips brushing my skin and sending a teasing whisper of an aftershock rushing through me. "*He* needs you."

I tried to open my mouth to ask what he meant, but my eyes slid shut and when I reopened them, I was lying face down in my bed in the alpha's residence.

My body throbbed with unsatisfied need because I

hadn't just had the most amazing sex of my life, I'd only dreamed it. That, and my back hurt a bit.

Right. Cyrus had yelled at me, there'd been blood, my blood, and then I—

I guess I passed out. Mid-yelling.

Swell.

I turned my head to see if he was sitting in the chair glaring at me again, the movement ratcheting up my need, making me hyper-aware of the fact that I was naked, and that heat and moisture pooled slick between my thighs. It would just be my luck that he'd want to continue his reprimand the second I regained consciousness, and that would probably just turn me on more.

The image of him completely naked, his large, powerful body on full display as he stormed toward me, flooded my mind's eye.

My inner muscles clenched and a low, needy moan, escaped my lips.

I squeezed my eyes shut fighting to regain some control over my body. *Please don't be in the chair. Don't be in the chair.*

I wasn't going to survive if he was. I'd beg him to have sex with me, but he'd probably just glare at me, which would turn me on even more because I was an idiot like that.

Fuck. I needed to get a hold of myself.

I cracked my eyes open, but thankfully the chair was piled with the clothes Bishop had bought me and not

Cyrus, saving me the embarrassment of throwing myself at him and ripping his clothes off.

Now to just spend the rest of my day... my life like this. Because my state of near-constant arousal wasn't natural.

Maybe I should have sex with Bishop. Just to take the edge off. He was still the best choice between him and Cyrus, but all the reasons for not sleeping with him were still there.

Which left me to deal with my desires myself, like always.

I turned to push the blanket aside to get up and go to the shower, but just that little movement sent another, more powerful tremor rushing through me. Another low needy moan fell from my lips and I collapsed back on the bed, already panting with need.

Embarrassment burned my cheeks, and I pushed my face into my pillow, trying to stifle the sound. The bathroom was just across the hall, but if anyone was waiting for me outside my door, they were going to know right away that I needed an orgasm, and they wouldn't even have to smell my arousal to know that.

If it was anyone other than Bishop or Cyrus they'd all think I was at the height of my first heat. And if it *was* Bishop or Cyrus... I didn't know if I'd be able to control myself.

The only way around this was to try and take the edge off my need so I could get into the bathroom and finish myself off properly.

I rolled onto my back, but not even the sting of lying on my injuries cut through my sex-induced haze. With a groan, I dipped a finger through my soaking wet folds and slid it over my clit. Just a quick one. That was all I needed. But the instant I touched myself, I melted into my touch and my fantasy turned into my dream... and to a very naked Cyrus.

BISHOP

I PRESSED MY BACK TO THE HALL WALL BESIDE THE DOOR TO Audrey's bedroom and squeezed my eyes shut, my cock so hard it hurt. Her arousal flooded my senses, and it took everything within me to stay on this side of her door.

Whil had discovered something about the mating bond, and I'd come to check to see if Audrey was finally awake so we could find out what. Except when I'd reached to open her door, she'd cried out in pleasure.

The sound had shot straight to my balls and turned me instantly hard, and I'd heaved myself against the wall to stop from rushing in to see what was going on, who she was having sex with.

But as I stood there, sucking in breath after breath that did nothing to ease the need thrumming through me because the air was rich with her scent, I realized no one was in the room. There were no other scents and the only sounds inside were her breaths and soft little mewls.

What was she doing—?

My cock strained against my fly.

Fuck me. I knew *exactly* what she was doing. She was getting herself off.

Relieving the pressure from the mating bond, more like it.

I knew it was strong. I could feel the bond in Knox even though he'd mostly blocked our twin bond. It urged him to claim her, but I hadn't realized it was so strong that Audrey had become desperate. She and Knox had only been mated for a few days, and while yeah, she could just be giving herself a little something because she wanted to, the mewls coming through the door were too desperate and her breath was too fast for something casual.

You could help her with that, my wolf rumbled inside me as he reached for the doorknob.

No. I jerked my hand away. Knox and I had shared a few women before and while matings with more than two people were uncommon in our pack, it wasn't frowned upon like in other packs or cultures, but I had no idea how the mating bond would affect him. Especially with him so determined to fight it.

If we couldn't break it, he and Audrey were going to end up crashing together, and I feared anyone caught in the middle, even me, was going to get torn apart.

Afterward... yeah, they might consider adding another mate to their bond, but not before.

And while I knew I didn't need to put my cock in her

to make her come, I didn't know if I'd be able to resist the temptation.

My wolf growled, heaving inside me trying to take over.

He certainly wouldn't be able to resist.

And not just because her arousal had been driving both of us crazy for two days now, but because we liked her. She resonated with something inside us. I wasn't sure what. Watching her cry in Whil's library, her body trembling with the fear that she'd been living with her whole life, had made my protective urges go into overdrive, and then I'd been unable to stop touching her during dinner. I *needed* to comfort her soul almost as much as I needed to comfort Knox's.

But Knox was avoiding everyone and pushing the issue with him that he needed physical contact to steady his soul would only make him retreat more, so I'd tried to steady Audrey's soul — and in turn my own.

Except I hadn't gotten steadier. I'd dreamed of her the last two nights... well, her and Knox. I'd watched them crash together, their passion wild and unstoppable. My wolf had rumbled his desire but strangely had been content to watch. Somehow, despite it being a dream and my fantasy, the dream-wolf-me knew Knox needed Audrey more than I did and that my time would come.

Last night's dream had been so hot I was surprised I hadn't come while I was sleeping. Knox had claimed her, dominating her with his lips and hands and cock, making her scream with pleasure until she was trembling and sated and the bond between them radiated brilliant golden light.

I'd wanted so badly to join them, to claim her as well, but my wolf held me back, saying over and over again that it wasn't time.

My subconscious didn't seem to care that I didn't know her. It had already decided it had seen enough and wanted her. And Knox bonding to her only made it better.

She released a loud shuddering moan, the sound shooting straight to my cock, and the scent of her arousal grew thicker. She'd come and from the sound of it hard, and all I could think about were my dreams and how my dream-wolf knew my turn to push into her hot wet sheath would come soon.

The pressure inside me exploded, shattering my control, and my cock swelled.

Fuck. I was going to make a mess in my pants then have to do the walk of shame through the house back to my room to change if I didn't do something quick.

I leaped into the bathroom, undid my pants, and jerked out my cock. My cum erupted from me before I'd fully closed the door, spurting onto the bathroom floor, the force of my release bringing me to my knees.

Oh, fuck.

My wolf snarled, his essence surging, and I struggled to control him.

Now is the time, he said as if he were my dream-wolf.

But reality and dreams were two different things and

as much as I wanted to add Audrey to my bond with Knox, for the three of us to mate in all the ways possible, that didn't mean that was what Knox or Audrey wanted. And *they* were the ones trapped in the mating bond.

But my wolf didn't give a fuck about respecting Knox's bond or how complicated the situation actually was. He wanted to storm across the hall, make her come again and again until she was drunk with pleasure and I was once again ready to drive my cock into her warmth.

Maybe Whil's news was that she'd found a way to transfer the bond to me like I'd suggested.

More cum spurted onto the floor.

Fuck, this was the orgasm that just wouldn't end and it pissed my wolf off to no end that I was wasting it on the floor and not inside Audrey.

Which was a whole other level of fucked up. He'd never wanted pups before, never, until this moment, cared who we slept with. We'd enjoyed the chase, the flirting, the fucking, but that was it.

It had to be the mating bond with Knox influencing my wolf and our most primal instincts despite him trying to block our connection. The feelings were too sudden. They had to be his— or rather his wolf's feelings for Audrey. His wolf had wanted to accept the mating bond when it had first formed and Knox had fought him and won... but how long would that last?

If my dreams were prophetic in any way — which they weren't — he wouldn't last long.

I stared at the puddle of cum on the floor in front of

me, my cock still semi-hard in my hand even though I'd just blown my load and then some.

I really hoped Whil had good news about the bond, either breaking it or transferring it to me. Because if it was anything else, I wasn't sure how long *I'd* be able to resist her. I didn't want to have sex with her if my feelings weren't real. It didn't matter that I'd had casual relationships and one night stands before, my wolf had decided that Audrey was different.

AUDREY

AFTER THREE POWERFUL ORGASMS, THE ICY HOLLOWNESS OF Knox's rejection was finally stronger than the thrumming compulsion from the mating bond and I felt almost normal getting out of bed and putting on one of the slip-off dresses so I could go to the bathroom and take a shower.

Bishop stood in the hall, leaning against the wall beside the bathroom door. His expression was hungry and his wolf-darkened eyes captured my attention the second I opened the door. He took a deep sniff, making my pulse trip with renewed desire and my cheeks heat with embarrassment.

"I can't help it," I murmured, wrenching my gaze to the floor between our feet. "Maybe I am going into heat."

God, wouldn't that just be my luck? But that would explain why it wasn't just Knox I wanted.

"Have you had a heat before?" Bishop asked, his voice

soft, low, caressing my senses like silk across my hyper-sensitive skin. "Do you know what it feels like?"

"Women in my pack don't have one until they have a wolf form." I clung to the doorknob, frozen in the door-way, my mind desperate to hide in the bathroom or back in my room, but my soul aching to grab Bishop by the shirt and drag him in with me.

"The bond might have set it off. Whil might be able to tell you." He took a large step away from me and the bathroom door. "She also has news about the bond."

My gaze jerked back up to his. "Can she break it?"

"I don't know." He swallowed hard and his eyes returned to their honey-brown color, his wolf retreating back inside him. "She can wait until you've had a shower and we've gotten you something to eat."

"Right." I hurried the few steps across the hall to the bathroom before I gave in to my desire to grab Bishop. But the second I opened the door, his fresh-cut grass scent swept around me, along with something deeper, richer, that made me instantly think of sex, and my desire overwhelmed the icy hollowness again.

"Oh shit," he hissed, freezing me in place in the doorway and making my pulse leap. "Your bandages. I should help you with them."

He cleared his throat and drew up close, his body heat and power rolling over me. I clung to the doorframe, determined to not move or look at him or anything other than stand there and let him help me.

He quickly tugged off whatever had been taped to

my back then retreated down the hall, and I hurried into the bathroom and closed the door, escaping from him.

Except I hadn't escaped from his intoxicating scent and now I was trapped in the bathroom with it, aching as if I hadn't just come — three times!

Oh, God.

I really hoped Whil had figured out how to break the mating bond or had a potion or spell or something that could deal with this insatiable need for sex.

I powered through a cold shower, not even bothering to turn the hot water on and not caring how my back stung, toweled myself off, then had to retreat past Bishop back to my room for a change of clothes.

When I stepped back into the hall fully dressed, Bishop's wolf was hidden deep within him and he looked like the friendly guy I'd first met. We went to the kitchen, grabbed some pastries and apples, and walked to the back of the alpha's grounds to Whil's cottage.

We entered through the greenhouse library door and headed to the seating area at the back where we found her, Cyrus, and a big, black wolf.

Knox.

Our eyes met and my breath left my lungs— hell, all the air vanished from the greenhouse, sucked out by the tension and yearning and aching need ignited in the space between us.

A churning, tearing mix of icy hollowness and blazing desire swirled inside me and my body trembled, trapped between the need to throw myself at him — even in his wolf form — and the need to run away.

"Sit," Cyrus commanded, his power wrenching my attention up from Knox, who sat on the floor in front of the couch, to Cyrus sitting on the couch. He pointed to one of the plain wooden chairs, and I plopped down on it before I could stop myself or even think of picking a different one.

Bishop shot Cyrus a dark look but didn't argue with him as he sank onto the cushioned chair between me and Whil. The fae woman sat on the floor among her piles of books where she'd been the first time I'd met her, making me wonder if the piles were just "part of the furniture." Except a few of the books were distinctly different from the ones the other day, indicating that this was how she organized herself while she worked.

A large tome sat on her lap, opened to a spot near the back, and I stared at it, hoping that if I focused on it, I wouldn't look at Knox... or think about him... or about last night's dream.

The book's pages were yellowed with age and the edges rough as if they had been made by hand and the text looked handwritten in a dark, red-brown ink.

Was that blood?

Nah, who wrote a book in blood?

"What are you doing with the grimoire found in one of the death gods' temples?" Bishop asked.

Shit, maybe it *was* written in blood.

She smoothed her hands across the pages and looked

at me. "I found this book in a market in Savaria three hundred years ago and bought it to keep it out of the wrong hands. I never thought I'd use anything within its pages."

I didn't like the sound of that. I'd been going on the impression that they weren't going to kill me. Cyrus had been furious that I'd fought that grimalkin because my death could have killed Knox or driven him crazy.

But what if they were just looking for a way to save Knox from the horrible side effects of a broken bond? If I died too soon, it would hurt Knox, but now that Whil had found a solution, they were free to kill me and end this madness.

"I ah..." I glanced back the way we'd come even though I couldn't see the door to the outside, my pulse suddenly racing. "I..."

"Stay," Cyrus snarled, his power locking me in my seat before I could think to run. "Let's hear what it is before panicking."

Bishop set a hand on my knee, his touch easing some of the fear but not all.

"No one is killing anyone." He turned his attention to Whil. "Right?"

"Sort of," she said. "You're not going to kill someone, but some*thing*. You're going to kill your bond." She opened her mouth, paused as if she was listening to something, then looked at Knox. "I'd say the most dangerous part is getting there. I can't say for certain how dangerous the spell is, but there's evidence in this tome that says it shouldn't kill either of you."

"Who?" Cyrus asked as if he knew what she was talking about.

I glanced at Bishop. He didn't look confused at all.

Swell.

Knox had said something with his telepathy and hadn't included me in the conversation.

"Knox and Audrey have to go," Whil replied. "They both need to be there for the spell to work. But they need to walk into the heart of one of the death god's lands, so a dozen hunters at least would probably be best."

Cyrus frowned. "The closest death god is north of Dark-weald, but that's still at least a nine day hike. We can't spare a dozen hunters. We need to figure out how the grimalkins got so close to town and if there are more of them. We'll need all the bodies we've got protecting Stonehaven."

"I'll go," Bishop said then shot Knox a hard look. "Better one of the strongest fighters than a dozen weaker ones."

"Two," Cyrus said, rubbing his face, looking exhausted. Had he stayed up all night dealing with the grimalkin attack? "Two of the strongest fighters. I'm not letting my younger brothers walk into a death god's lands by themselves."

Right. Because I didn't count. I wanted to be upset about that, but I couldn't deny reality. If those grimalkins were an indication of how dangerous this world was, I wasn't going to be helpful on this trip. The best I could hope for was to not get in the way and not fuck up when it came time to do the spell to break our bond.

And really, I should be ecstatic. Whil had found a way to break our unwanted mating bond without killing either of us— or at least it *shouldn't* kill either of us. If it worked, I'd no longer be in a constant state of arousal, and the frozen emptiness inside me that threatened to shatter my soul would be gone.

I'd finally be able to live whatever kind of life I wanted.

I just had to walk into the lands of a death god and murder my bond. How hard could that be?

Don't miss the next book in the series!

Wolf Denied
Ensnared by the Pack: Book Two

I must break this unbreakable bond... no matter the cost.

The last thing I want is surly Knox taking our accidental mate-bond out on me. It's not like I asked to be bonded to the one man who wants nothing to do with me. But he won't even talk to me and the aching emptiness of his rejection is eating away at my soul.

Why couldn't I have bonded to his brother, Bishop? He's kind and sweet and there's something between us. I can feel it every time our eyes meet.

But I can't do more than look. Sleeping with my bond-mate's brother can only end badly. For us all. Especially not now when we've found the one slim chance to break this cursed bond. A slim chance I'm willing to stake our lives on. Even if it means traveling through a treacherous wasteland, fighting off dangerous monsters, and casting a spell that could kill us.

I can't fight this mate-bond forever and soon I'll give in to the torturous desire. The spell is my only hope...

Because there are some things worse than death.

OTHER BOOKS BY TESSA COLE

THE NEPHILIM'S DESTINY SERIES

Destined Shadows, prequel story

Destined Darkness, book 1

Destined Blood, book 2

Destined Fire, book 3

Destined Storm, book 4

Destined Radiance, book 5

THE ANGEL'S FATE SERIES

Fated Bonds, book 1

Fated Winter, book 2

Fated Fear, book 3

Fated Despair, book 4

Fated Resolve, book 5

Fated Heart, book 6

THE GRECIAN GODDESS TRILOGY

Kiss of the Goddess, book 1

Power of the Goddess, book 2

Bonds of the Goddess, book 3

ENSNARED BY THE PACK